"I would like you, ~~Mr. Mayor~~, members of the council, to appoint someone, perhaps one of your police officers, to look into the murder of Mrs. Talley. Neither James Talley nor his twin brother was ever tried or convicted of her killing. It happened a long time ago. Perhaps at that time there was fear of people like the Talley brothers. Perhaps the police just seized on these unfortunate twins and made them scapegoats. Perhaps there's something in the records that would show they couldn't have done it."

"Why doesn't she do it?" It was Walter Harris, the angry man in the front row. "Our cops don't have time for this stuff. It's her idea, so let her do it." He turned around and looked me in the eye.

"How 'bout it?" the mayor asked.

I was stunned. Suddenly on the spot, I found myself fumbling for excuses. "I'll be glad to," I heard myself say, wondering who was behind the voice coming out of my mouth. . . ."

By Lee Harris
Published by Fawcett Books:

THE GOOD FRIDAY MURDER
THE YOM KIPPUR MURDER
THE CHRISTENING DAY MURDER
THE ST. PATRICK'S DAY MURDER
THE CHRISTMAS NIGHT MURDER
THE THANKSGIVING DAY MURDER
THE PASSOVER MURDER
THE VALENTINE'S DAY MURDER
THE NEW YEAR'S EVE MURDER
THE LABOR DAY MURDER
THE FATHER'S DAY MURDER
THE MOTHER'S DAY MURDER
THE APRIL FOOLS' DAY MURDER
THE HAPPY BIRTHDAY MURDER

THE
GOOD FRIDAY
MURDER

Lee Harris

FAWCETT BOOKS • NEW YORK

A Fawcett Book
Published by The Ballantine Publishing Group
Copyright © 1992 by Lee Harris

www.ballantinebooks.com

Library of Congress Catalog Card Number: 91-93154

ISBN 0-449-14762-2

Manufactured in the United States of America

First Ballantine Books Edition: April 1992

10

For my mother
who's read them all

A man's real possession is his memory. In nothing else is he rich, in nothing else is he poor.

ALEXANDER SMITH

The author wishes to thank
Ana M. Soler and James L. V. Wegman,
without whom this book could not have been written.

1

I still wake up at five in the morning.

It's hard to break habits practiced for fifteen years, especially when those fifteen years are half your life. Five o'clock comes and my mind starts to work, setting sleep aside. It had been three weeks since I left the convent, three weeks since I established myself in Aunt Meg's house—which would be mine as soon as the will was probated—but 5:00 A.M. still worked its powers on me.

I turned over, looked at the clock, and closed my eyes, hoping sleep would work its own magic, but it failed again. It was nearly the first day of summer and the sun had risen at its earliest. After fifteen fruitless minutes of trying to sleep, I got out of bed and went to the bathroom, automatically opening the medicine cabinet as I entered so that I would not see myself in the mirror. During the years that I had visited Aunt Meg once each month, she had dutifully taped a carefully cut cardboard cover over the mirror before my arrival. But the prohibition, like the early awakening for morning prayers which I no longer said, still maintained its hold on me. I had not looked at my reflection since the day I left St. Stephen's, although nothing but custom prevented me from doing so. Everything in its own time, I told myself.

My morning washing completed, I pulled the medicine chest shut as I left the bathroom and returned to my bedroom. On my arrival three weeks earlier, I had chosen to sleep in the room Aunt Meg had set aside for me rather than the one she had shared with Uncle Will for so many years and then occupied alone after his death. The master bedroom was considerably larger than the one I had chosen, but I knew why I was not yet ready to enter it. It was not the idea that it had been hers and she was only three months gone. Rather it was the large mirror over the dresser in which I had once glimpsed myself years ago and, shamefully at that time, lingered to see my face and figure, an infraction I had confessed to a priest upon my return to St. Stephen's.

Now I opened the closet in my old room and saw again the yellow silk dress hanging on the inside of the door, the hanger hooked over the top of the door. I had gone on a necessary buying spree when I left the convent, purchasing skirts, blouses, dresses, and pants, and had picked the yellow dress because I was enchanted with its daffodil color and fluid texture. But I had not yet been able to bring myself to wear it.

"Too warm for silk," I said aloud, and pulled out Old Faithful, a pair of khaki slacks and a short-sleeved white camp shirt, both of which had been washed and ironed half a dozen times since their purchase. A pair of crew socks and sneakers finished my outfit and I was ready for my morning outing.

I'm not an exercise fiend or a health nut, but I enjoy a brisk walk or jog in the early morning. It makes a nice substitute for morning prayers and builds an appetite, which seems sensible since I don't wake up hungry. Halfway down the block I ran into a woman about my age who was walking off a pleasing plumpness.

"Good morning," I called, measuring my pace to hers.

"Hi. Are you the new neighbor?"

"I guess I am." I held out my right hand without breaking stride. "Christine Bennett. Call me Chris."

She grasped my hand in a firm handshake. I like that. "I'm Melanie Gross. Mel. We live at 507."

We ran in tandem for a minute or so, turning right at the corner.

"You aren't Margaret's niece, by any chance, are you? The nun who always came to visit?"

"I am, but I'm not a nun anymore."

"I see."

She was probably being tactful, asking no questions, ruffling no feelings.

"There's no secret about why I left," I volunteered. "I made the decision nearly a year ago and my permission came through in April. I stayed on to finish the semester. I taught English at the college."

"Really?" Mel smiled broadly, almost with relief. "I had no idea. Margaret never mentioned . . . A teacher. Will you be staying on in the house?"

"I hope to. I'm very fond of the house, and it's mine now."

"Well, that's really nice. Are you coming to the meeting tonight?"

"What meeting?"

"The last council meeting of the year. They're taking the vote, you know. Or maybe you don't know. Whether to let that group house into town. You ought to be there. It'll probably be one of those knock-down-drag-out affairs, till the wee hours, I expect. Would you like to drive over with Hal and me?"

"Thanks, but I wilt at night. If I decide to go, I'll take my own car so I can leave before the weest of hours."

We turned another corner and I could see Pine Brook Road just ahead. "I'm going back," I said, moving away from her. "See you later."

" 'Bye, Chris. I have to give it fifteen minutes more."

Fifteen minutes later I was just setting out my cholesterol-laden breakfast of eggs, buttered toast, a couple of sausage links. I ate it all with relish.

It was five weeks to the day since I had last visited my cousin Gene. Gene was the reason for my monthly visits to Aunt Meg, the reason she kept a room for me all those years. On the third Monday of every month I would drive from St. Stephen's to Oakwood, have dinner with Aunt Meg, sleep in my room, and visit Gene the next day. My teaching schedule was arranged to accommodate the monthly trips, and I had been granted permission to own a car so that I could make the trips without using the trains, thereby saving myself hours of travel time. Oakwood was nowhere near the train that came down along the Hudson.

Gene was one year older than I, born when Aunt Meg and Uncle Will had been married almost fifteen years, Aunt Meg on the eve of her fortieth birthday. He had been born retarded, a sweet, loving, handsome boy who would never grow up to be the doctor or lawyer or schoolteacher everyone else's son would become. At an early age I had realized that Gene wasn't like the other children I knew, and my mother had explained it to me allegorically. For Aunt Meg and Uncle Will, Gene had not been an allegory. As much as they loved him, he had been a constant trial. He could never be left alone. After a certain age, he could not even be left with an ordinary baby-sitter. When Uncle Will died nearly ten years ago, Aunt Meg could no longer cope. Tearfully she put Gene in Greenwillow, an institutional home some ten miles from Oakwood. But the good news was that Gene loved it.

I drove over after lunch. I had changed into a plaid shirt-dress and exchanged the morning's sneakers for sandals. The yellow silk had beckoned to me when I opened the closet door, but I had declined once again. I didn't need silk to visit my cousin Gene.

Greenwillow was housed in a wing of an old hospital which had been spiffed up some years ago for the occupants and now sorely needed a respiffing. I parked the car in the area reserved for visitors and walked to the door. As I approached, I had an unexpected attack of something like anxiety. I had never walked through that door without my habit on, never been addressed by my birth name by the staff. Probably, I thought, that's why I had put off this first post-convent visit. There had been no reason to wait for today to see Gene. In fact, now that Aunt Meg was gone, I intended to visit him frequently, as she had done.

I rang the doorbell and waited for someone to open the heavy door. It was Clarice, one of the aides, who came.

"Hi," I said. "I'm here to see my cousin, Gene Wirth."

She looked at me oddly and I felt a little guilty. "He's up in his room. Do you know where it is?"

"Sure. Thank you." I escaped her puzzled gaze as I walked to the stairs.

The door to Gene's room was open, and I stood in the doorway and watched him for a moment. He was sitting at the table where he kept his collection of tiny cars. He had been collecting them for as long as I could remember, and in my bag I had a new one for him, as I usually did when I visited. He moved them in a careful, deliberate way, lining them up, then selecting two to travel side by side down an imaginary road.

"Hi, Gene," I said, stepping into the room.

He looked up, momentarily startled, looked at me piercingly, then broke into a smile. "Kix," he said, and I felt tears come to my eyes.

Someone, probably my mother, had tried, when we were very young, to get Gene to say "Chris." He hadn't been able to wrap his tongue around the sounds and it had come out "Kix," a name that had remained forever my nickname to my most intimate friends. When I had first begun visiting him dressed in my habit, Gene had been terribly confused. He could not associate the habit-clad woman with his cousin. Once I had even pulled off my veil to show him who I was, but he remained unconvinced. Sometimes he would ask where Kix was, and it was clear to me that it was quite unclear to him where indeed I was.

"Kix is here," Gene said. He stood up, his face beaming.

"I sure am." I went over to get my hug.

"Where's Mama?"

"Mama's gone to heaven, Gene. Remember we talked about that last time I was here?"

"Don't remember."

But he did remember; he just didn't want it to be so. We sat down, he on his chair next to the car table, I in the easy chair.

"I have something for you."

"A car?" He brightened up again.

"A very special car." I dug it out of my bag and handed it to him.

He looked at it and touched it and played with it. Then we settled back to have our visit.

An hour later, Gene accompanied me downstairs. I knew many of the residents by name and I stopped to say hello to some. Eventually they would get used to me, as Gene would. At the bottom of the stairs I ran into the custodian, sweeping up with his broom and pan.

"Hello, Alex," I said, pausing.

He looked at me, bringing me into focus with narrowed eyes. I was about to tell him who I was when he said, "You look like that Sister Edward used to come here."

"I was Sister Edward. I've left the order, Alex. I'm Christine Bennett now."

He pursed his lips and nodded. "You sure look like Sister Edward."

"I'm—"

He interrupted. "You Gene's cousin, too?"

"Yes, I'm Gene's cousin."

"You got a lotta nice cousins, Gene," Alex said, but Gene wasn't paying attention.

"I'll be visiting regularly from now on," I told Alex. "I'm sure I'll see you around."

"You see our famous murderer?" Alex asked, cackling.

I wondered if I had misunderstood. "Your famous what?"

"The poor old fella who's causing all the trouble. Over there." He indicated an easy chair near the fireplace.

A gray-haired man sat rocking softly, his eyes somewhere on the ground.

" 'Bye, Kix," Gene said. He had spotted a small group and now made his way toward them.

" 'Bye," I called after him. I turned back to Alex. "You say that old man over there—"

"Killed his mother. Stabbed the life out of her." He shrugged. "That's what they say. I don't believe a word of it. He's just a nice old gentleman, sits by himself, don't bother no one.''

"He looks harmless enough." I was intrigued. "What's his name?"

"James. Don't bother trying to talk to him. He won't answer. Just ask you where his brother is."

"Where is his brother?"

"I dunno."

"I'll see you next time, Alex."

I walked away to where I could stand and watch James. He had an extraordinary head of white hair, which was bent and moved slightly as he rocked himself. I thought I saw his lips moving, but I could hear nothing.

I took a wooden chair and pulled it over to where James sat. "Hello, James," I said.

If he heard me, he kept it to himself. The rhythm of his rocking never changed.

"My name is Chris," I said. "My cousin Gene lives here. I visit him."

The man rocked. Now I was certain his lips were moving, like a nun's in silent prayer.

"Have you lived here long?" I asked. "I don't remember seeing you before."

"Do you know where my brother is?" he asked, speaking very quickly, not moving his head.

"No, I don't. What's your brother's name?"

More rocking.

"If you tell me his name, maybe I can find him."

The rocking stopped, but nothing else changed.

"I'll say hello to you the next time I come to see my cousin Gene," I said. "Okay?" I stood and picked up my handbag.

James made a sound and I stopped. "Did you say something?"

"Robert." He spoke without moving, his eyes still fixed on something on the floor.

"Is Robert your brother's name?"

"Robert," he repeated.

"Thank you, James. I'll see if I can find him."

2

I had not quite reached the front door when a woman's voice called, "Sister Edward."

I turned to find the director of Greenwillow standing before me. "Mrs. McAlpin." I held out my hand.

"It is Sister Edward, isn't it?" she asked hesitantly, shaking hands.

"It's Christine Bennett. I left my order at the beginning of the month."

"I see. I wonder if you'd step into my office for a moment."

I followed her into her attractive, comfortable office and took a chair. She sat behind her desk, a handsome woman with an air of toughness about her.

"I understand you're taking over Gene's guardianship," she said.

"I am."

"Allow me to say that I'm delighted. He couldn't have a more concerned guardian than you." She smiled, and I wondered what she had invited me in for. Now that I was to be my cousin's guardian, I would be told when he misbehaved, would be consulted on changes in therapy. "The attorney said I could reach you at Mrs. Wirth's house in Oakwood."

"My aunt left me the house. I'll be living there."

"You're the only person from Oakwood with a connection to Greenwillow."

I had no idea why that fact might be worthy of mention, so I smiled foolishly and waited.

"Surely you know about our plans?" Mrs. McAlpin said.

"What plans?"

"Our plans to move Greenwillow to Oakwood. There's a wonderful old house we hope to renovate for our special needs."

I was flabbergasted. Aunt Meg had taken several buses in each direction for all those years to visit Gene, and now Gene was coming home to Oakwood. "That's wonderful," I said. "Gene'll be a neighbor."

"Only if the Oakwood Council approves us."

"Why wouldn't they? You're quiet, you don't play loud music, you don't have all-night parties. You won't even use the schools."

Mrs. McAlpin smiled patiently. "I see being cloistered has kept you out of touch with some of society's modern battlegrounds. No one wants a group like Greenwillow next door or down the block. People imagine our residents are potentially violent, and no amount of medical testimony can convince them otherwise. In our case, there's a special aspect to their objection."

"What's that?"

"We have a new resident here, James Talley, who has been unfairly tarnished with the blame for a violent crime."

"I was just speaking to James before I ran into you."

"Speaking to him?" She sounded mildly disbelieving.

"A word or two. What's he supposed to have done?"

"Killed his mother."

"How long has he been here?"

"Nearly three months. He was incarcerated in a high-security institution for nearly forty years. It took that long to bring about a determination that he was no longer dangerous. If he ever was."

"He told me he had a brother."

"A twin brother, Robert. They're both what's called 'idiot savants,' although James is no longer a savant. They had wonderful abilities at one time, but James lost his long ago."

"And James murdered his mother?"

"No one will ever know. Perhaps James did it, perhaps his brother did. Perhaps they did it together. More likely, an intruder came in. By the time Mrs. Talley's body was found, any evidence there might have been had been completely destroyed by the twins.'' She paused meaningfully. ''The body wasn't found for several days. You can imagine what a mess that house was.''

''I can.''

''And it was convenient or expedient to assume the twins were guilty. Sister—Miss Bennett.'' Mrs. McAlpin looked across her desk earnestly at me, and I knew she had come to the reason for our little chat. ''Greenwillow needs your help, quite desperately, in fact. We have tried every means at our disposal to persuade the town of Oakwood to accept us. The father of one of our residents gave us the services of his advertising firm so that we could place informative literature in the hands of every resident in town. We sponsored an evening question-and-answer session, which seemed to be going well until a group of very vocal and very hostile people took over, undoing much of our work. The final vote of the council is tonight. I no longer know where we stand. I'm afraid the vote will be very close. Now that you're a resident of Oakwood, you can speak for us. Several very wonderful people have done so already, but we can use another voice.''

''I'd be happy to speak. I'm really very grateful to you for telling me about all this.''

Mrs. McAlpin's executive face broke into a smile. She rose, walked around the desk, and took my right hand in both of hers.

''Thank you. Thank you so much. We really want that house. It has everything Greenwillow needs, space inside, land outside. I'm very grateful to you, Miss Bennett.''

I stood and shook her hand. For a moment I thought she might kiss me. ''I'll do my best,'' I said.

''That's all we can ask.''

3

The monthly meeting of the Oakwood Council began at eight. Anticipating a crowd, I drove over half an hour early. The parking lot was already filling, and inside the firehouse, the seats up front were already taken. I found an empty chair in the fourth row and sat.

The mayor called the meeting to order a few minutes after eight. By then every seat was filled and a handful of people were standing along the side aisles. The firehouse wasn't air-conditioned, but a woman had set several fans going in the front and back of the large room. I was glad I had kept the shirtdress on; anything else and I would have been sweltering.

There were several obligatory rituals to be performed at the outset, and I sensed the impatience of the spectators as the minutes were read and approved and some rather boring old business was taken care of. Finally, about nine-fifteen, the mayor addressed the main issue.

"We have a question before us," he said, moving papers this way and that as though he could not quite remember what the question was. "Resolved: That the town of Oakwood grant a variance of statute 703 to permit the group known as Greenwillow Associates to buy the property at 411 Central Avenue, known as the Aldrich property." He looked up, his mouth set. "Are there any comments for or against?"

The number of hands raised, people rising from their seats, shouts of "Yes, right here," took me by surprise. It seemed that everyone present had something to say. My first reaction was to be thankful that I had napped in the afternoon, giving

me, I hoped, the strength to stay awake for what promised
to be a long night.

The mayor recognized a man in the front row. "State your
name and address for the record, please."

The man, already on his feet, said, "Walter Harris, 37
Mill Road." Then, without taking a breath, he continued.
"I would like to state in the strongest possible terms my
unalterable objection to allowing Greenwillow to buy the
property in question or any other property that may in the
course of time come on the market in Oakwood. As you all
know, I have nothing against the retarded. We've gone over
and over the dangers that exist to the people themselves,
dangers from cars tearing down Central Avenue, danger of
drowning in the brook that runs behind the Aldrich property,
all kinds of dangers. I won't go into all of them again. That's
the problem of the Greenwillow Association, not our problem. If they think they can cope with all of that, more power
to them." I noticed he was glancing at notes he held in one
hand, and I wondered if we would be out of here before
daylight. "But our problem—and I mean the problem of every
man, woman, and child in Oakwood—is who they let live in
that house. We can't have a convicted murderer in our midst
even if he didn't murder anyone for forty years. You can't
ever tell with people like that."

"Point of order, point of order!" a woman shouted from
the rear.

"What's your point of order?" the mayor asked wearily.

"No one in that house is a convicted murderer. Mr. Harris
knows that. Everybody in this room knows that."

The mayor banged his gavel. "That's not exactly a point
of order, Sally," he said. "You better sit down and let Walter
finish."

"You can't let him spout lies, Mr. Mayor," the woman
shouted.

"Walter," the mayor said, "try not to spout lies. Okay?"

"You bet," the man in the front row said, and continued
his tirade.

When he sat down, someone jumped up and asked for a

motion that all discussion be held to two minutes. The motion was soundly defeated. A second motion was made to limit discussion to four minutes. That one passed.

I did a little quick arithmetic. If a hundred people spoke, we would have nearly seven hours of discussion before the question came to a vote. They would carry me out. Or perhaps I would just lie down on several of these very uncomfortable wooden folding chairs and sleep—after the vote.

I sat and listened for almost three hours. It was encouraging that a determined group of people, all sitting together on the other side of the room, were solidly in favor of letting Greenwillow into Oakwood. They brought up just about every point that I had noted on a pad this afternoon, but certainly it would do no harm to repeat them in my own words.

What seemed clear from the negative contingent was that they had largely abandoned the rather silly objections that Walter Harris had begun his oration with—the "dangers" to the Greenwillow residents, obviously a collective euphemism for people's fear of having a group of retarded adults in their midst.

Instead, they had latched on to the murderer in the group. As I listened, I found myself completely out of sympathy with their position. To believe that the quiet, sad man sitting in the chair in the Greenwillow lounge could have killed his mother, could have used a weapon as intimate as a knife to draw her blood, required more imagination—or less information—than I had. I didn't think James Talley could be angered to the point of wanting to kill, much less make the attempt.

But these people believed it, and the belief was making them afraid. In the years I had known her, I had often heard my spiritual director, now the Mother Superior at St. Stephen's, say, "You may be smarter than they are and you may know more than they do, but that's no excuse to patronize them." And on one occasion she had said, "If they believe something, that's reason enough to respect it." Just because I wanted Greenwillow to have the house on Central Avenue, just because I wanted Gene nearby in a better home, I couldn't dismiss these people's specious arguments and real fears, however much I disagreed with them.

I decided the time had come to speak up. I would reiterate a point that had been made before and I would make a suggestion. There were still hands raised, still people rising and making their feelings known, and it was already past midnight. If I didn't get my chance soon, I might lose what little energy I had left.

I raised my hand.

The mayor recognized two people before he pointed at me and said, "State your name and address for the record."

I rose. "My name is Christine Bennett, and I live at 610 Pine Brook Road. I'm a new resident in Oakwood. My aunt, Margaret Wirth, passed away and left me her house in this lovely town, and I intend to live here and be an active participant in town affairs. This afternoon I visited Greenwillow." I let them draw the obvious conclusion, that I had been exercising my right as an active participant in town affairs by making the visit. "While I was there, I met James Talley."

There was an actual gasp and then a stir among the diehard spectators. "He is very quiet, very docile, and I felt no fear whatever during the time I spent with him."

"It doesn't matter!" someone shouted, and the mayor banged his gavel and shouted back, "Let the lady speak. You had your turn."

"I understand your apprehensions and your misgivings. Someone accused of a murder and never cleared of it is someone we find hard to trust, even after many years and after exemplary behavior. James Talley was given permission to reside at Greenwillow because for almost forty years he has shown no sign of a violent nature."

"But tomorrow he'll kill someone," a man behind me called out, and the mayor gaveled him down.

"I would like to make a proposal to this town and this council. I'd like you to delay your vote until your next meeting. When do you meet next, Mr. Mayor?"

"Third Tuesday in September."

"You've only got a minute to go," the timekeeper warned.

"Let her talk." This from a member of the pro-Greenwillow group across the center aisle.

"I would like you, Mr. Mayor, members of the council, to appoint someone, perhaps one of your police officers, to look into the murder of Mrs. Talley. Neither James Talley nor his twin brother was ever tried or convicted of her killing. It happened a long time ago. Perhaps at that time there was fear of people like the Talley brothers. Perhaps the police just seized on these unfortunate twins and made them scapegoats. Perhaps there's something in the records that would show they couldn't have done it."

"Thirty seconds."

"Miss—uh—Bennett," the mayor said, glancing at his scribbled note, "our police force, as you may not know, is very overworked and understaffed. For one of our officers to devote the time that such an investigation would require—"

"Why doesn't she do it?" It was Walter Harris, the angry man in the front row who had kicked off the discussion. "Our cops don't have time for this stuff. It's her idea, so let her do it." He turned around and looked me in the eye.

"Good idea," one of the pro-Greenwillow people across the aisle called, and then there was a murmur of general agreement.

"How 'bout it?" the mayor asked.

"Time's up," the timekeeper said.

"Oh, sit down, Doris," the mayor grumbled.

I was stunned. Suddenly on the spot, I found myself fumbling for excuses. I had a course to prepare for; I had volunteer work I wanted to do. "I'll be glad to," I heard myself say, wondering who was behind the voice coming out of my mouth.

The hands of half the people in the room were raised.

"Sonny Terry, 151 Maple. What if she finds out nothing? What if it's all a wild-goose chase?"

I was still standing and I spoke without being recognized. "I will turn over all my information, whatever it is, to this council before the start of the school year. The council can vote as it wishes.''

"Let her do it," someone called.

"Yeah."

"It's another damned delay."

The mayor banged and banged. A hand was raised and a resident was recognized in the midst of the chaos. As the noise abated, I heard a motion proposed with my name in it.

"So move," a councilman said.

"Second."

"Call the question."

The secretary read the motion, editing it as she read. The mayor called for a vote.

To my surprise, the vote was unanimous. In favor. I had been appointed to investigate the Talley murder and turn over the results of my investigation to the mayor and council before the September meeting. My heart was pounding rather wildly and I was about to make a fool of myself.

"If there is no other business," the mayor droned.

People were standing, moving up the aisles, coming toward me. I found myself shaking hands, being thanked, being invited to visit.

I was so tired, it was all I could do to find my way to the car, drive home, and get myself to bed.

4

I slept right through till six, a first in my adult life, having exhausted myself the night before. I dressed and went out for my morning exercise, too late, apparently, to run into Melanie Gross. I was happy to be alone. When I had made my offer earlier this morning, I had done so without thinking of the consequences. Where had the Talley murder occurred? Might I have to fly to California or Montana to peruse police records? Although I had a comfortable income, it would not pay for such extravagances.

The phone started ringing before nine, just as I finished cleaning up my breakfast dishes. Happily, the first call was from Mrs. McAlpin.

"Miss Bennett," she said, her businesslike voice almost emotional, "what a fine thing you've done. When I asked you to speak in our behalf, I never imagined anything quite so generous."

I didn't want to say it hadn't exactly been generosity. "It seemed the right thing to do and the right time to do it. The people who don't want Greenwillow have practically abandoned all their other objections. If I can bring some persuasive evidence that James Talley didn't kill his mother, I think the council will accept the group and forget all those lesser gripes. But I'm going to need your help to get started."

"Anything," she said. "Anything at all. And as soon as you're ready."

"I can be there in half an hour. I would appreciate it if you would try to find out all you can about where and when the murder took place."

"I'll do that directly." She hung up so abruptly that I almost felt slighted.

"Mrs. Talley was probably murdered on April seventh, 1950, in an apartment in Brooklyn, New York."

I felt a surge of relief as she said this. Midtown Manhattan and Brooklyn were both about twenty miles from my Westchester County suburb and easy to reach by car.

"I must tell you, Miss Bennett, the day it happened was Good Friday."

My heart did a little blip at that, but I said nothing.

"The body wasn't found until two days later, that is, the ninth, Easter Sunday. The twins had been alone in the apartment with her the whole weekend."

"Do you know who found the body?"

"I don't, no. But the murder was front-page news, most especially in the tabloids. I'm sure you can find microfilm copies in many libraries, although probably not in Oakwood's. I have other information for you as well. The Talley twins were well-known within the medical community. I believe I told you yesterday that they were savants. While they could scarcely add two and two, they could somehow come up with successive prime numbers of great length. Although you don't recall that period of time yourself, I can tell you that computers were few and far between and much less sophisticated than they are today. Testing prime numbers the Talleys produced sometimes took mathematicians days of work. But they were always correct.

"And they had other gifts, too," she went on. "They could remember every day of their adult lives, what they ate, what they wore, what the weather was like. Today poor James can't even tell you what he had for lunch."

"You said he lost those gifts."

"Sadly, yes. He's been in a high-security facility upstate since the judge remanded him there. The atmosphere, as you can imagine, is as far from Greenwillow as prison is from a private home. We had hopes, when he arrived, of seeing those gifts restored. Unfortunately, in the months he's been here, there hasn't been any noticeable progress."

"And where is his brother, Robert?" I asked.

"I'm afraid I don't know that. Certainly not in the upstate facility that James was in. It's possible that my contact at New Hope will know. I'll call today." She made a note on a pad in front of her.

"What about the father, Mrs. McAlpin? There must have been a Mr. Talley."

"So there must, and that's something else I don't know. Perhaps the newspapers will say."

I looked at my watch. It was ten o'clock. There was more than half a day during which I could work. I stood and started to say good-bye.

"Miss Bennett," Mrs. McAlpin said hesitantly, "I don't

know quite how to say this. I don't know what your financial circumstances are, but if you run into difficulty, I'm sure I can find—''

''Thank you, but that won't be necessary. When I left the convent, I received what was left of my dowry, and Aunt Margaret named me as her sole heir. She was far from rich, but she left what seems to me to be a very substantial sum, as well as a house without a mortgage. And I'm quite used to going out with fifty cents in my purse.''

Mrs. McAlpin looked concerned. ''That's only two phone calls nowadays. I'd put some folding money in that bag of yours. Just to make me feel happy.''

''I'll do that.'' I started for the door and stopped. ''Is James Talley Catholic?'' I asked.

''Let me see. Yes, I believe he is. He's taken to mass every weekend.''

''Thank you. I'll keep in touch.''

5

By ten-thirty I was driving south to New York. My first stop would be the public library on Fifth Avenue at Forty-second Street. I had no idea where I would park, but I assumed something would turn up. I had fifty dollars in my wallet, more cash than I had ever had on my person in my life.

Mrs. McAlpin's concern about my finances had been a good and generous one, but in my case, misplaced. When I had entered St. Stephen's that terrible, rainy night fifteen years ago, I brought with me my inheritance of twenty thousand dollars, more money than I had ever heard of, but not much as inheritances go. A few months later, a check for my mother's life insurance of ten thousand dollars was forwarded to me and added to the dowry. Some of that money had been used to buy the first year's toiletries that a novice must supply herself—soap, toothpaste, hand lotion, and other personal necessities. Later, when I was given permission to own a car, the dowry had paid for it and had subsequently paid for gas, oil, and periodic maintenance.

But the car was used little aside from the monthly trip to Oakwood, and bank interest covered the car's expenses. There was still a sizable chunk on deposit when I left the convent.

In September I would start to teach at a local community college. The letter from the chairman of the English Department still brought smiles when I reread it:

"As part of our continuing effort to offer a wide range of courses by a staff of diverse backgrounds, I am pleased to offer you the position of associate to teach Poetry and the Contemporary American Woman."

The idea of teaching poetry had filled me with sheer delight, but if Professor Caldwell thought that fifteen years in a convent teaching English to nuns and secular women in a Catholic college qualified me as a contemporary woman, I had to wonder at his judgment. But I was so thrilled at the offer that I had telephoned my acceptance and followed it with a letter that I had personally mailed at the post office the following morning.

The pay was probably low for college teaching, but for me, it was bountiful. It would more than pay for a winter wardrobe and probably take care of my utility bills as well. I was ecstatic.

The cost of parking my car left me dumbfounded. Mrs. McAlpin had been right to warn me. Lunch took another unexpectedly high toll. In future, I would take a sandwich with me on my travels. My former vow of poverty would stand me in good stead for my summer's work.

But the microfilm of the newspapers gave me so much

information that I quickly forgot about the expense of acquiring it. EASTER MASSACRE! the Monday front-page headline of one tabloid shrieked at me. "Retards Slash Mother," the subheadline at the bottom of the page continued. I moved the screen to the next page.

BLOODY APARTMENT YIELDS GRISLY SECRET, the inside headline read.

Retarded twins James and Robert Talley, 29, apparently slashed their mother to death in the kitchen of their Brooklyn apartment over the Easter Weekend, leaving bloody fingerprints in every room. Horrified police, acting on a phone call, entered the apartment before noon yesterday to find the body of Mrs. Alberta Talley, 61, on the floor of her kitchen, her throat slashed and multiple stab wounds throughout her body. "Only a madman could have done this," police Detective Kevin O'Connor said as the body was being removed from the apartment. The murder weapon was believed to be a serrated bread knife about ten inches long which was found near the body. The twins, whose hands and clothes were stained with blood, were nearby.

I began taking notes in the steno book I had taken with me, but soon abandoned the task. I was able to make hard copies of the microfilm by positioning the screen to the section of the page I wished to copy and depositing quarters. A reader in the reference room and a helpful librarian added to my supply of coins, but the librarian admonished me to bring plenty of quarters with me next time. I agreed to do so.

I read days of articles in the first newspaper, then moved on to other papers to see if any one of them might have a different slant or some new nugget of information. I was surprised at the number of papers available in New York in 1950. The *Herald Tribune* was still alive, as were others I had never heard of: the *World Telegram and Sun*, the *Journal-American*, and the *Daily Mirror*. It became a task of diminishing returns, but by the time I felt that I was finished, I had accumulated a collection of names, dates, times, and suspicions. When finally I looked at my watch and saw that it was nearly five o'clock and felt an incipient headache from staring for so many hours at the screen, I gathered my papers and notes, returned the last film, and went to ransom my car.

At home, I ate quickly and sat down in the dining room, which I had never used and could be conveniently converted to a makeshift workroom. I took a package of typing paper, the photocopies of the newspapers, my steno notebook, and some pencils and pens. On the first page of the notebook, I had printed a favorite line from Keats: "Heard melodies are sweet, but those unheard are sweeter." As always when I read it, I felt the poet speaking directly to me. I smiled and began my work.

On a page of typing paper, I started a chronology of events, beginning with the morning of Friday, April 7, 1950.

At a little before nine, as she always did on Mondays, Wednesdays, and Fridays, young Magda Wandowska, an immigrant from a Baltic country (variously described by the papers as Estonia, Latvia, and Poland), arrived at the apartment of Alberta, James, and Robert Talley. She would spend three hours cleaning the apartment, allowing Mrs. Talley the freedom to leave, to shop, occasionally, it appeared, to have her hair done (as she did that morning), without having to worry about the welfare of her sons. "They were good boys," Magda was quoted as saying in two of the papers, a somewhat amusing comment because the "boys" were eleven years older than she.

It was an ordinary morning. She cleaned up the kitchen and chatted with the boys. Mrs. Talley put her hat on and left a little after nine. She had a nine-thirty appointment at the beauty parlor—in honor of Easter, Magda explained— and then she would shop for food and return home.

During her three hours, Magda took the boys for a walk along Ocean Avenue, where their apartment house was. (One paper mentioned that Mrs. Talley paid $74.50 for the two-bedroom apartment, and I was not sure whether that was a great deal or practically nothing, but the reporter seemed surprised at the amount.) The three of them walked to Quentin Road, over to East Seventeenth Street, and up to a park that was a favorite spot of theirs. There they sat and talked and played the kinds of games the boys liked to play, word and number games that gave Magda the feeling that, although they were not normal in the sense that they could function in society (she didn't use those words), they had been selected by God for greater gifts. On that day Magda asked them about the day she had been born eighteen years earlier (in one of those Baltic countries), and they had told her the weather—in Brooklyn—what they had eaten for lunch, and the color of Mama's dress (purple). Even though she had been born some five thousand miles away, it had given her a closeness to the boys, knowing they remembered the day.

About eleven-thirty they had started back, this time going along Avenue S to Ocean Avenue, a slightly longer walk, but they were in no hurry. Mrs. Talley had arrived promptly at noon with her bags of groceries and her freshly coiffed hair and had paid Magda for the week, nine dollars for the nine hours (a generous sum for the time), and thirty cents for carfare. Magda had promised to return on Easter Sunday to help Mrs. Talley take the boys to church—not that she needed help, the boys were so good, but it didn't hurt to have an extra person along. Generally when they went to church, Mrs. Talley would sit at one end and Magda at the other so that the boys were enclosed between them. Magda never accepted payment for attending church with the Talleys, which was only about once a month; it was her gift to God. But Mrs. Talley always gave her ten cents for carfare and often placed a dollar in the collection basket, a princely sum for the time.

When she left the Talleys, she went to church for Good Friday services. The Talleys would not go. Services were long, and the boys sometimes became restless.

Magda spent the evening quietly with her parents and sister. On Saturday she had a special job cleaning a house for a lady who was having a large group over for Easter Sunday.

She was paid well, but she worked hard and she came home tired.

Easter Sunday morning, she dressed and took the bus to Ocean Avenue and Kings Highway.

Magda had the key to the Talley apartment. It had not started that way. At the beginning, when she was still in high school and came to work a few afternoons after school, Mrs. Talley would give her the key so that she could go walking with the boys. But Mrs. Talley sometimes forgot, preventing their outing. Finally, when a great deal of trust had grown between them, Mrs. Talley had given Magda her own key, and that was how she got in that terrible Easter morning.

She had rung several times and could hear footsteps inside, but no one answered the door. Perhaps, she thought as she stood waiting, Mrs. Talley was in the bathroom, readying herself for church. The boys had been told never to answer the doorbell, much as one would caution a child, and Magda knew they would be obedient. And since it didn't really matter whether Mrs. Talley opened the door or whether she let herself in, she took the key out of her bag and used it to enter the apartment.

She could see that something was wrong the minute she got in. The twins were there, disheveled, dirty—she didn't realize it was blood until later—and when they saw her, they began to cry.

"Mama, Mama," one of them said.

"What happened?" Magda said, frightened. "And then I thought," one of the newspapers quoted her, " 'Mother of God, Mrs. Talley has had an accident.' I ran to the bathroom, thinking she had fallen."

But Mrs. Talley was not in the bathroom. There was blood in the bathroom, in the sink and on the tile floor and on the towels. More frightened than ever, Magda ran to Mrs. Talley's bedroom. It was neat, the bed made as it always was— "She was such a clean person," Magda told the police—but Mrs. Talley was not there. She ran into the boys' room, which was in disarray, the beds not made, blood on the sheets. But no Mrs. Talley.

Magda then ran through the living room into the kitchen and stopped herself at the door. There it was. "It" was the ravaged body of Alberta Talley, lying on the kitchen floor, covered with blood, blood congealed on the floor about it, blood on the cabinets, blood splashed on the window and the pretty white curtains.

"I crossed myself," Magda said.

It must have been horrible. Reading the accounts, I wondered that so young a girl had comported herself so bravely. First she took Robert by the arm and walked him to Mrs. Talley's bedroom. She told him to stay there and closed the door. (She explained that Mrs. Talley sometimes locked one of the twins in her bedroom when she was too busy to look after both of them. Magda didn't have the key to the bedroom, but, she said, she thought Robert would believe he was locked in and would stay there. He did.)

She then called the police. They came very quickly, she said, and they were very kind.

I put all this into my chronology and then looked further for reports of the autopsy and the questioning of possible suspects. The autopsy reports were in the Wednesday papers, having been made public on Tuesday. Mrs. Talley had died of multiple stab wounds covering almost all her body. Some of them were fairly superficial—as if the killer didn't mean it, one newspaper said—but the slash across the throat was probably the mortal blow.

Fingerprints from James and Robert Talley were found everywhere—on the bread knife that had killed their mother, in the blood that had congealed on and around her body, and throughout the apartment. Both twins had handled the knife; in fact, they had held the blade as well, leaving me to believe that they had picked it up out of curiosity or horror but not as a weapon. The police removed the twins from the apartment in handcuffs. There were photos of them being led away. I could not tell one from the other in the pictures, but I could see the resemblance between the twenty-nine-year-old twins and the old man at Greenwillow.

I suppose the police questioned them for hours, perhaps

overnight. The year 1950 was long before the famous Miranda case and the subsequent Miranda warnings that everyone nowadays takes for granted. Heaven only knows how they abused those two poor young men, but apparently to no avail. Neither twin admitted anything. In fact, they were quite silent, asking frequently for "Mama" and for each other.

The tabloids kept the story alive in that grotesque manner that is not common nowadays. I KNEW THEY WERE KILLERS, one headline screamed on Wednesday, quoting a neighbor who lived in another building on Ocean Avenue and who sometimes saw the twins walking with Mrs. Talley or Magda. There was little behind the headline, and I felt disgusted both by the sentiment and by its publication. I am not always a lover of the good old days.

Separate from my chronology, I made a list of all the people mentioned whom I thought it would be useful to interview. There was Magda, of course, if I could find her. There was Sergeant Kevin O'Connor, who had told one newspaper that only a madman could have done such a killing. I hoped he had been young in 1950 so that he might still be on the force or perhaps retired somewhere in the area. There were people living in nearby apartments who were mentioned by name. I knew that New York's rent-control laws made it disadvantageous to move, and I thought there might just be a slim chance that someone who remembered that Easter Sunday might still live in the same building. And I wondered very much about the missing Mr. Talley.

I had a lot of work ahead of me. Before going upstairs to get ready for bed, I tidied the dining table but left my notes and microfilm copies in separate piles, neat and accessible. I had more questions than answers. Tomorrow I would begin to ask them.

6

I hooked up with Melanie Gross the next morning and we walked, ran, and talked.

"I was there Tuesday night," she said as we rounded the first corner. "Do you really think you can find out anything about a murder that happened so long ago?"

"I don't know, but I've already started and I've learned a few things."

Melanie broke into a smile. "You did? When? What have you done?"

"I spent yesterday at the New York Public Library reading old newspapers on microfilm."

"That's fabulous. Have you got anything?"

"Just a deeper respect for the Miranda warnings."

"Oh?"

"Those twins were questioned for hours without a lawyer. I'm sure you know what that means."

"Was there a confession?"

"I don't think they ever got anything out of them. I'm going to Brooklyn today to see if I can dig up the file on the case. I'd like to see whatever records there are of the questioning, and I'd like to see the autopsy report."

"Will you be able to read it?"

"Probably not, but I'll take it to Aunt Meg's doctor, who's also my cousin Gene's doctor. I'm sure he'll help."

"Listen." Mel slowed her pace, and I slowed my own to stay even. It's tough to run and talk at the same time. "I'd like to tell you how I feel about Greenwillow."

"Sure."

27

"If James Talley isn't in the group, I have nothing against the house being in Oakwood. I frankly wouldn't want it next door to me, because we'd never sell the house. But I don't object to their buying the Aldrich property. It's the possibility of that man being a murderer that stops me. I have children and I'm concerned about their welfare. You don't have to have kids to understand that."

"Of course."

"If you really find that someone else did that murder—and I can't imagine how you can do that—I'll support the variance."

"Thanks, Mel." We had come to a stop in front of my house. "I really appreciate your support. And I'm going to come back for it in September."

"You'll get it. But not if there's still a cloud over Talley's head. Okay?"

"Okay." I waved as she jogged down the street to her house. It was time to start fighting clouds.

I drove down Ocean Avenue before I went to the police station. It was a wide street with old apartment houses, most of them about six stories high, and interspersed here and there with a one- or two-family house. Young mothers pushed strollers, and older men and women hobbled along with canes, walkers, or companions for support. The building the Talleys had lived in was of the same vintage as the others, probably a once grand place to live.

I drove slowly along the great avenue, crossing Quentin Road and then Avenue R and Avenue S. They had walked up the street—I wondered on which side—forty years ago, not knowing their mother would die horribly that afternoon or evening. The autopsy report estimated the time of her death as "sometime on Good Friday," not a very scientific conclusion. Someone even linked the brutal murder to the crucifixion. I found that hard to believe.

A car honked behind me, and I put on some speed and found the Sixty-fifth precinct.

* * *

Outside, the police station looked like every picture I had seen on television or in the movies. (We watched TV at St. Stephen's sometimes in the evening.) Inside, there was a high counter with a stone front, wood top, and stainless steel railing separating me from the uniformed people on the other side. One of them was a woman, and she asked politely if she could help me.

"I hope so. I'm looking into a murder that took place in this precinct forty years ago."

I don't know what I expected, but what she said left me almost speechless.

"Sorry, can't help you," she said, voice and expression dismissing me.

It was such a complete turndown, I didn't know how to proceed. "Do you think someone else could help me?" I asked finally.

"No." She turned away and spoke to a male officer.

I waited for her to return, but she obviously thought she had done with me. "Excuse me," I said a little loudly. "I really need some help."

She came back. "Ma'am, there's no one here who was even alive forty years ago."

I looked around and had to agree with her. "There have to be reports, records," I persisted. "I want to see the file."

She took a deep breath and exhaled to show her irritation. "Maybe the desk officer can help you." She pointed to my right. "Ovuh theah."

"Thank you very much." I smiled to show I was grateful and went to the designated desk. A police officer was sitting there, and if the woman I had just spoken to had sounded weary, this one looked on the verge of sleep. He glanced at his watch as I approached.

"Good morning," I said as cheerily as I could manage.

"What can I do for you?" the officer asked.

"My name is Christine Bennett," I said.

"Ah-hah," he responded automatically.

"And I'm looking into a murder that happened in this precinct forty years ago."

He practically rolled his eyes. "Ah-hah," he said as I spoke.

"It's very important, Officer—" I glanced at the name tag just below his badge "—Korb."

"Ah-hah."

I was somewhat disconcerted. "The men who were thought to be guilty of the crime—"

Officer Korb was shaking his head. "See, lady," he said, interrupting me finally with a new syllable, "we don't even have the records for that in this building. This building wasn't here forty years ago."

"But surely those—"

" 'Scuse me," a voice behind me said. "Is this something the squad can help you with?"

I turned to see a kind of nice-looking guy about my age in a sport jacket.

"I don't know," I said.

"Whyn't you give it a shot, Sarge?" Officer Korb said, relief all over his tired face.

"Hi, I'm Sergeant Brooks." He stuck out his free right hand and we shook. "Come on upstairs."

We went up to a room filled with desks, mostly men and a couple of women working at them. There was an empty one at the far end, and Sergeant Brooks hung his things up, took off his jacket, and made himself comfortable at the desk, while telling me to do the same.

"Officer Korb's a little overworked," he said with a grin that let me know Officer Korb had never been overworked in his life.

"I could see that."

"What seems to be your problem?"

Here we go again, I thought, psyching myself up for another try. "Believe it or not, I'm looking into a murder that happened in this precinct forty years ago, and I'd like to see whatever records the police department has on it. I can give you names and dates and—"

I had hoped to say enough that he would be unable to turn

me down flatly, but he stopped me. "Whoa, hold on. *When* did this happen?"

"April 7, 1950. The victim's name was Alberta Talley."

"Alberta Tally." He wrote on a piece of folded paper.

"E-Y," I corrected him, reading his writing upside down.

"Oh, sorry." He scratched it out and wrote it over. "Can I ask why you're interested in something that happened forty years ago? Did it involve a relative of yours?"

"No. It was a murder without a conviction, but two people have spent forty years in a prison atmosphere because it was thought that they did it. I don't know whether they did or not, but I need to find out. Something very important depends on it."

"Okay, tell me about it."

"Now?"

"Sure. Talk. They pay me to listen."

I said, "Thank you. Today you'll earn it."

He was a good listener, and I told him almost everything I knew, as well as why I needed the information. He took notes in a spiral pad and asked occasional questions, and I drew a sense of confidence from that. When I finished my recitation, I sat back in my chair. "That's it," I said.

"Okay." He tapped his pencil on the desk twice. "I think I can find that file for you, but I can't do it now. It's not in this building. Files that old are in the borough headquarters. I'll go down there and hunt them up."

"You will?" I must have sounded incredulous.

"I'll give it a shot and see what happens."

"Will the autopsy report be in the file?"

"A copy should be."

"That's great." I felt as though I were already halfway there.

"Better give me a call tomorrow before you come down. What borough do you live in?"

"Borough? Oh, you mean New York. I live in Oakwood."

"You came down here from there for this?"

"Yes, and I'll be back as soon as you find that file."

"Here's my card."

I looked at it. Sergeant John M. Brooks. "I'm Christine Bennett. Can I call you at nine?"

"I'm on ten to six tomorrow."

"Thanks." I stood and offered my hand. "An awful lot," I added as we shook.

I drove back to Ocean Avenue and had the kind of luck New Yorkers always hope for. As I coasted down the street, my eyes peeled for a parking space, someone pulled out and I had one. It was still too early to eat lunch, and my sandwich and can of soda were safely cold in Aunt Meg's plastic picnic box packed with a bag of ice. I left it in the car and found the Talleys' apartment house.

I must admit to a certain feeling of discomfort at the thought of ringing bells and knocking on the doors of strangers. Part of that was, I think, an ordinary fear of being considered a little weird. Most people alive today weren't born forty years ago, and I would probably encounter more people—many more—who didn't remember the Talley murder than would. But the other part of my reticence was, I'm sure, a product of the way I'd lived for the second half of my life, all my adult life until three weeks ago.

I hadn't been cloistered as Mrs. McAlpin had assumed. In many ways I was an ordinary teacher of English literature in a college for women. I met the parents of my students and spent lovely hours walking, talking, and dining with the girls I taught. I knew what problems they had, because they confided in me. But at this moment I felt sorely deficient in what they call interpersonal relationships. Talking to strangers was not, as my students would have said, my bag.

But there was no other way. I entered the small foyer of the Talleys' building and looked around. There was a bank of mailboxes on the left wall, and another bank on the right. In front of me was a pair of double doors made of glass panes, heavy wood, and fairly shiny brass. But the door was locked.

The only way to enter was with a key or by being buzzed

in by a tenant. I didn't know any of the tenants, and I was not about to ring bells and hope someone would push a buzzer. Maybe some other time, but not today.

I went back out into the sunshine. Across the street were three private houses wedged between two large apartment buildings. The houses seemed much less threatening, and I crossed the street and went to the nearest one.

A child answered my ring and called her mother, who quickly informed me that they had lived there for only seven years, and the tenants upstairs for two. But, she added helpfully, there was a very old man next door who had lived there a long time.

I thanked her, went down the stone steps and up those of the adjoining house. These houses were so close together that there wasn't room between them to park a car, although one of them had what looked like a narrow driveway. It had probably been built in the days when cars were a lot smaller than they are today.

All three houses had tiny front lawns, but this house had rather elaborate plantings as well and a Japanese red maple in the center of the lawn. Someone obviously cared and put time into gardening.

My ring was answered by a middle-aged woman in a housedress. She looked at me with that mixture of curiosity and apprehension that I was to find frequently in New Yorkers who encounter strangers.

"Good morning," I said. "My name is Christine Bennett and I'm looking into something that happened in this area in 1950. I know that's a long time ago, but I wonder if you or anyone in your house might remember and be able to help me."

She sized me up for a long moment. "You mean the murder?" she asked.

I felt a surge of hope. "The Talley murder, yes."

"I was very young at the time," she said, and I knew she didn't want to tell me how old or I might figure out her age. "My father would remember it better than I would."

"I would be so grateful if you would let me talk to him, and to you, too, if you wouldn't mind."

She thought about it. "Who did you say you were?"

"Christine Bennett. I can show you some identification." I took my wallet out of my bag and pulled out my driver's license, glancing at it as I did so. I stopped, holding it in midair. The picture showed a smiling nun.

Before I could withdraw it, the woman had taken it from my hand. "Oh, you're a nun. Come in, Sister."

I had a quick attack of conscience. The last thing I wanted to do was deceive. "I'm not a nun anymore," I admitted, hoping I wasn't destroying my chance to talk to her father. "I've left the convent."

"I see. Well, come in. I'm Mrs. Cappicola, and my father's name is Antonetti. Wait here and I'll get him."

She walked off with my license, and I remembered Aunt Meg saying that Italians were such good gardeners. It was a stereotype I thought they might be proud of.

Mrs. Cappicola returned a few minutes later with a small old man with white hair and a white mustache. We said hello and she handed my license back. The three of us sat in the living room.

"You wanna know about the murder?" the old man asked from his easy chair.

"Yes, please."

"You wanna tell me why?"

"I'd like to find out if the twins really did it."

"They went to jail, didn't they?"

"Yes, but there was no trial, and I'm not sure there was much of an investigation."

"I think they done it."

"You do."

"Yeah."

"Did you ever see them, Mr. Antonetti?"

"Oh, sure. Saturday and Sunday they used to walk sometimes on the street. I was a young man then, forty-four years old. I didn't sit in the house and look out the window like I do now. But I saw them."

"Were you afraid of them?"

"Not for myself, no. But for my wife and daughters, sure."

"I was afraid." It was the daughter.

I turned to her. "Why?"

"They didn't look—right."

"But did they ever do anything to make you afraid? Did they grab at people or talk to people in the street or fight with their mother?"

"Nah," the father said. "They walked, one on this side o' her, one on that side. That's all."

"I used to see them with the girl sometimes," Mrs. Cappicola said. "The blond girl. She's the one that found them."

"Were you here when the police came?"

"We was in church," the old man said. "It was Easter. We come home, the whole side of the street was filled with blue-and-white police cars."

"I saw them carry the body out," Mrs. Cappicola said in a low voice. "I never saw anything like that ever again. I saw them take those twins out. They had handcuffs on." She shook her head. "To think something like that happened right here."

"You didn't happen to know Mrs. Talley, did you?" I asked.

The old man smiled. "There's a million people livin' in those buildings. They're all strangers. Every one of them."

I had only one more question. "What about the father? Did you ever see him?"

The old man shrugged, and his daughter pursed her lips and shook her head.

"Wasn't no father," Mr. Antonetti said. "I read that in the papers."

"Thank you." I went over and shook his hand. "I appreciate the time you've given me."

"Well," the daughter said, "I hope it's been a help."

I assured her it had and left them, but I didn't think it had done me much good. I went to the last of the three houses and rang the bell, but no one was home. It was time for lunch, so I went back to the car and ate my sandwich.

7

I am a persistent person. With half a day left and a strong desire not to waste time, I returned to the Talleys' apartment house. It was true there was no way in other than to ring bells at random or wait for someone to come in or out and hope to gain access that way, but there was also a superintendent in the basement apartment. I rang that bell, got an almost immediate buzz, and took the elevator down one flight.

A woman in her forties or fifties—I am notoriously bad at guessing age—opened the door. "Hi," she said in an almost friendly way. "If you're looking for an apartment, we're full up and there's a waiting list."

"It's a beautiful building," I said. "I love the brass in the lobby."

I had obviously said the right thing. She smiled. "I take care of that myself."

"I'm not looking for an apartment today. Actually, I'm looking into a murder that happened here in 1950."

"Oh, that big one, where the twins did it."

"Yes, that's the one. You're much too young to remember it yourself, but I wonder if you know of anyone in the building who might have been living here at the time."

"Well, let's see." She thought for a moment. "Come on in while I check."

"Thank you." I went into a small living room and waited. The woman disappeared and came back with a book. "I got all the tenants in here and when they moved in. What year was that again?''

''Nineteen fifty.''

''Nineteen fifty. This'll take a minute.'' She put her glasses on, opened the book, and started turning pages. ''Would you mind telling me why?'' she asked, looking up.

''I have an interest in the twins, the sons of the murdered woman.''

''The ones that did it, you mean.''

''Well, the ones they think did it.''

''You mean maybe they didn't?''

''I really don't know.''

''Hmm.'' She went back to the book. ''Here's one, Selma Franklin, 4C. Lived there since 1938.''

I was truly amazed. ''You mean she's lived in the same apartment over fifty years?''

''Guess so. She's told me a million times, she moved in as a bride, raised her kids, buried her husband. 'They'll carry me out,' she said. And they will. She ain't movin' for nobody. They'd love to get her out, if you know what I mean. Beautiful two-bedroom. They could get a mint for it. But she's a senior citizen; they can't budge her, can't raise her rent. Here's another one, Annie Halpern, 6E. Moved in in 1948. She don't hear so good now.''

I was writing it all down, feeling encouraged.

''I thought there was more, but I guess that's it. A lot moved to Florida, and a bunch of them died since we got here twelve years ago.''

''I wonder, would you take me to see one of those women? Maybe Mrs. Franklin, since her hearing is better.''

''Yeah, I guess I could.''

I realized I should reward her for her trouble. I took a ten-dollar bill out of my wallet and handed it to her. ''I'm really very grateful to you,'' I said.

''Aw, you don't have to do that,'' she said, taking the ten.

''That's all right.''

''Come on. We'll try 4C.''

* * *

Selma Franklin was a tiny, round woman whose face was always on the verge of a smile. She was so happy to have company, to have someone to drink tea and eat cookies with her, that I felt if I learned nothing from her, the time spent would not be a waste.

The living room was immaculate, beautifully furnished, with family photographs on nearly every horizontal surface. The more than fifty years of memories were well documented, and I felt myself in the company of a happy woman.

"Eat, darling," Mrs. Franklin said when I sipped my tea but took nothing from the tray of cookies.

"Thank you." I took a cookie and bit into it. It was delicious. "You must have been expecting me," I said.

"I expect, they come. People are always coming. I have friends, neighbors. The children are all coming by."

"I can see why."

"You want to know about the murder?" The superintendent's wife had explained the reason for my visit.

"Whatever you remember."

"Everything," she said. "Like it was yesterday. The police, the sirens, the reporters asking everybody questions. Who would expect such a thing to happen on the next floor?"

"Did you know Mrs. Talley?"

"We would say hello. We lived in the same building for twelve years, after all. She would walk her children, I would walk mine. 'Hello, Mrs. Talley, I see you're out with the children,' I would say, and she would say, 'Hello, Mrs. Franklin. Look at how your boy is growing.' That's how we talked."

"How did the boys act with her, Mrs. Franklin?"

"Quiet. Good behavior. They looked around. They walked. I didn't see them talk much."

"Were they ever—" I hesitated "—violent?"

The round face broke into a wonderful smile. "They were quiet boys. There was a little something wrong with them, that's all." She reached over to offer the tray. "Have another cookie, darling."

I took one, just to keep her going.

"You know, in my husband's family there was one like that, a boy, a nice boy, but he didn't grow up. He stayed a child. He had a good heart. He would draw pictures. They even got him a job later, delivering messages. He always had a smile, that boy. You couldn't be afraid of him. And those twins, they were *good boys*. If she said, 'Say hello to Mrs. Franklin,' they would say hello. If she said, 'Robert, what color is the light?' he would say, 'Green,' and she would say, 'Then we can cross the street.' "

"Then you must have been very surprised to hear they murdered their mother."

"Listen to me, sweetheart, the police have got to find someone. You go in an apartment, there's a dead woman and two poor sons with blood all over them, it looks like they did it. When did you ever see the police overwork themselves?"

"So you think it's possible they didn't do it."

"What does it matter what I think?" She got up from her deep chair and poured both of us more tea. "I love a cup of tea," she said.

"It matters," I said to her, and when I saw the puzzled look on her face, I added, "It matters to me what you think."

"What I think is that they didn't look too hard and they didn't find anyone else, and they had these two poor children who touched everything in the apartment the way children do and they couldn't explain anything, so that was that. What else I think is that someone else could have done it."

"But who would that have been?"

"This I can't tell you. There was a little blond girl that worked there—she found the body. Who knows? Maybe she has a fight with Mrs. Talley. Maybe the super comes up and tells Mrs. Talley he doesn't want those boys there anymore. The super in those days—I don't remember his name anymore—he wasn't the nicest person in the world. So maybe there's an argument. Maybe the gas man came to read the meter and took the elevator up to find an empty apartment to rob. You think such a thing never happened? Somebody rings and one of the twins opens the door and poof! She's dead."

Almost as she said it, her doorbell rang. She lifted herself from the chair, went to the door, and called, "Who's there?"

"Andy," a small voice came back.

Mrs. Franklin opened something in the door, looked out, then turned the lock and opened the door. A little boy scampered in.

"Andy," Mrs. Franklin said, scooping him up and kissing him. "I knew you were coming, I have cookies." She put him down.

He looked at me shyly, found the cookie tray, and took two. "My mommy says hello."

"And hello back to your beautiful mommy." Mrs. Franklin was beaming.

They chitchatted for a minute and then Andy said good-bye and left. Mrs. Franklin locked the door behind him.

"You see," she said, still standing at the door, "when someone comes, I look through the peephole." She tapped it with her finger. "But when it's a little fellow like that, you can't see him."

"So if Mrs. Talley let someone in, she knew who it was."

"Absolutely. But if one of the twins did it, who knows?"

"The newspapers said the twins didn't open the door, that they were trained not to."

"Sweetheart," Mrs. Franklin said, "let me tell you about the newspapers. Those reporters came to every apartment. They asked every question you could think of. And you know what they did then? They went back and wrote their stories out of their heads. They said Mrs. This and Mrs. That said such-and-such. They said no such thing. It was all made up. Nowadays you have television. You ask a question, you see the person giving an answer. But in 1950 who had television? I can tell you, after it happened, I never opened the door again without I looked first."

"I have just one more question," I said, setting down my cup of tea. "Do you remember Mr. Talley at all?"

"Mr. Talley? There was no Mr. Talley. Not from the time I lived here."

"How can you be so sure? You lived on a different floor. He might have left early and—"

"Sweetheart, I'm telling you. No Mr. Talley. My best friend, Harriet Cohen, may she rest in peace, lived next door to the Talleys."

"I see." I stood and went to shake her hand.

She pulled herself out of the chair again. "You'll take a couple of cookies with you for later," she said.

"Well, I—"

"They shouldn't go stale." That was to tell me what a big favor I was doing her.

She made me promise I would stop by if I ever came back, and I took her telephone number in case I thought of any more questions.

Then I left. As I started for the elevator, I heard the distinct sound of the bolt being turned in the heavy door.

There was still time to talk to the other woman who had lived in the building in 1950, but I thought better of it. The person I needed to talk to was Magda Wandowska. And I hadn't the slightest idea of how to find her.

8

On Friday I decided to start the day by trying to talk to James Talley. When I arrived at Greenwillow, Mrs. McAlpin intercepted me and we talked in her office for about a quarter of an hour. She's a woman with a controlled, low-key managerial style, but she was pretty excited at what I told her, convinced that it was progress. When I asked for permission to speak to James Talley, she escorted me to his room.

It was a room similar to my cousin's, but the furniture was

arranged differently and the curtains and bedspreads were a different color. Mrs. McAlpin left me, and I stood just inside the door.

"Hello, James," I said.

He was sitting in his easy chair, and he looked up at his name.

"My name is Chris. May I come in?"

He didn't say anything.

I walked in and sat in the desk chair. "We met a few days ago. Do you remember?"

He nodded his head. Then he said, "Do you know where my brother is?"

"I don't know, James, but I'm trying to find out. I'm trying very hard." I watched his face for some glint of acknowledgment of what I'd said, but I couldn't see any. Then I plunged in. "Do you remember Magda, James?"

This time there was a definite response. The head bounced up and the eyes seemed almost to glow.

"Do you remember when Magda took you and Robert for a walk?" I asked softly.

He said, "Magda."

"Yes, Magda. She was a very nice girl, wasn't she?"

But I had lost him. He turned away, deep in his own thoughts, if indeed they were thoughts.

I wondered what kind of melodies James Talley heard.

At ten-thirty, after I had said hello to Gene, Sergeant Brooks answered his phone.

"Got it," he said when I gave him my name.

"The file? Really?"

"Right here in front of me."

"It'll take me an hour."

"I'm here all day."

I enjoy driving. My monthly trips to Oakwood were a special joy for all the years that I made them from St. Stephen's. There was something about being alone in a car, being the captain of my own ship, that I found satisfying.

Now, driving to Brooklyn to see the file on the Talley murder. I thought of Frost and the road not taken. But I thought of it happily. The road that I was traveling right now was that road, and I was taking it.

There were things I missed that I had left behind at St. Stephen's, good friends, a way of life rich in fulfillment. I remember the first time I saw the convent, before I entered it, when I went up as a visitor. It was awesome, as the young girls say now, big and heavy and very beautiful, on landscaped grounds shared with the college in which I would later study and even later teach. There was a warmth from the nuns, a girlish friendliness from the novices.

"And you know," one of them said as we toured the grounds, "we have such a lovely view of the Hudson River."

I couldn't see it, but I didn't want to say so, afraid that I would unwittingly insult my guide. Later, when I myself was a novice, I realized it was a joke. "The view of the river" that everyone mentioned now and then, especially to visitors and prospective novices, didn't exist. It was all a myth. Even in winter, when every branch was bare and the air cool and dry and you could see for miles, there was no river.

Once, I had climbed to the top floor of the Mother House and stolen a look out the windows that faced west. There was no river. It had saddened me to know it, but I had kept the secret. The nuns would have their jest.

"I went through it this morning," Sergeant Brooks said, indicating a thick file tied with string that lay on his desk. "I have to tell you, I had some funny feelings reading it."

"What do you mean?"

"Well, there were some loose ends I didn't like. Maybe somebody could have worked a little harder."

"Maybe it wasn't necessary." I heard myself become the devil's advocate. "Maybe the twins were just guilty and that was that."

"I don't know. I think if it had been my case, I would've followed up on a couple of things."

"What kind of things?" I tried not to sound too eager.

"For one thing, the knife."

"Why?"

"Let me show you." He opened the top desk drawer and pulled out a twelve-inch ruler. "Here's a knife you're about to stab me with. Show me how you hold it."

I took it in my right hand and wrapped my fingers around it. "Something like this."

"I can see you're no pro. It's got to go in this way." He turned my clenched hand so that the ruler was horizontal. "Gets stuck in the ribs the other way. Very messy. But look at where your fingers are. They're more on the edge than on the flat surface. But the prints on the cards are nice, clear, whole prints. And some of them came from the blade."

"I read that in one of the papers," I said, feeling a ripple of excitement. "I had a feeling the twins might have picked it up to look at it out of curiosity, not to use it."

"That makes two of us. And there was something else. I thought they should have followed up a little better on other people that might have visited the apartment, maybe some guy hanging around the building that might have followed them upstairs."

"The gas man," I said, remembering Selma Franklin.

"Like that, right. But you can't look into things like that forty years later."

"I understand. But there are people with names that might still be living."

"Possibly." He looked at his watch, and I was afraid he would tell me he had other things to do. "Why don't we go out to lunch and talk?"

"Thank you, I have a sandwich in the car."

"Leave it for supper. C'mon." He pushed his chair back and stood.

"I guess I could."

"Sure you can." He started walking, pausing at an occupied desk to say something quick.

When we were out on the street we walked two blocks to a small restaurant and went inside. The waitress knew him and teased him about not having been around for a while.

I read the menu. When the waitress came for our order, I said, "Tuna fish on rye, please, with lettuce and tomato."

Sergeant Brooks stopped her from writing and turned to me. "That's what you've got in your car for supper. Live it up a little."

I'm sure I blushed. He was exactly right about what I had in my car. "Eggplant parmigiana," I mumbled, and sipped a glass of ice water. "And a glass of iced coffee," I added before she took the sergeant's order.

Frankly, I was about as nervous as I've ever been in my life. I was sitting at a table with a man I found attractive in a very nice way. He had a ready smile, an easy manner, curly hair that I expected defied both brush and comb and looked as if it rarely saw either, rather pale eyes that didn't avoid mine but invited confidence. He had been kind to me. He had helped me in ways I could not have helped myself.

And in all of my thirty years I had never found myself in—don't laugh—so intimate a situation. I was close enough to touch him, I who did not touch men. But I think I realized then for the first time in my life that when a man and a woman are near each other, the idea of touching arises quite naturally. It didn't do much to calm me.

When the waitress had left, he felt in a couple of pockets and then pulled out a much-folded piece of paper—it turned out to be several sheets—and started to unfold it. He had written on many of the folded surfaces so that as he talked, he had to turn it this way and that to retrieve information. It seemed to me a disorganized and inefficient method of taking notes, but to my surprise, he found what he was looking for very quickly. So much for organization.

"I've been through the highlights of the Talley file," he said. "It's pretty clear the guys working on the case were sure who did it the minute they walked in that apartment. And there's a lot of reason to think they were right. But as I said at the precinct, it's possible they were wrong. If they were, I have to tell you it's an almost impossible task to prove anything at this point."

"But we can explore some possibilities," I said.

"We can explore anything."

"We talked about the gas man. That's one of the possibilities, isn't it?"

"It always is. A guy gets in the building for some legitimate reason—he reads a meter or delivers a package—and then looks around for an apartment to burglarize. He could've gone up to the fifth floor, rung the doorbell, gotten in, and killed her. But there's a lot wrong with that."

"Tell me."

"First of all, he killed her with her bread knife. Guys don't carry bread knives, and the one that was used was identified by the girl who worked for her." He looked at his notes.

"Magda," I said.

"Right. Wandowska. And suppose the gas man did it. Why didn't he steal anything?"

"You mean nothing was missing or disturbed?"

"Disturbed, yes, but by the twins. Missing, probably not. There was jewelry in her dresser, some good stuff, a diamond ring. And there's something else. A guy like that doesn't stop with one. Sooner or later he's caught and they match his fingerprints with others where the MO is the same."

"But they were sure they had a killer here."

"True, but they would've tried anyway."

"All right," I said, setting aside the gas man theory, not unhappily, because it was unprovable. "Suppose Magda did it."

"An eighteen-year-old girl knifing a woman to death?"

"It's not impossible."

"It's pretty farfetched."

"She said she left at noon on Good Friday and went to church. Maybe she killed Mrs. Talley before she left. She knew no one was coming back till she was expected on Sunday. They could have had an argument. Maybe it was unintentional."

"But you're forgetting the twins," Sergeant Brooks said. "Magda knew the twins. She knew they were savants, that they would remember everything that happened."

''That's true. I hadn't really thought of that.''

''So she couldn't take a chance of having them tell what they saw. Which pretty much rules out anyone who knew the twins' powers.''

''So we're back to the gas man.'' We said it almost in unison and then we laughed.

''Now, as it turns out,'' Sergeant Brooks went on, ''the twins never said anything. If they were guilty and they understand what they did, I can see why. But if they're not guilty, why haven't they ever said anything? There was no statement, no denials, nothing.''

''They were traumatized,'' I said.

''I can buy that. But what I can't buy is someone knowing in advance that they would be.''

''Which, as you said a minute ago, rules out anyone who knew them. It leaves me with a very tough job.''

''They may have done it.''

''They were described as almost docile.''

''I'm not a psychiatrist,'' Sergeant Brooks said, ''but I've seen cases where normal people went berserk. Can you rule out that a retarded person could do the same?''

''Of course I can't rule it out. But I've spoken to James Talley twice, and he seems a man of sadness, not a man of anger.''

''But he's been traumatized, remember? He's not the same person he was before his mother's murder.''

''I think that's true,'' I said, starting to feel discouraged. But discouraged is not defeated. ''I need to find Magda,'' I said. ''The law of averages says she's still alive, and my head tells me she hasn't forgotten any of what happened.''

''You want to see her even though you think she might be guilty of murder?''

''I don't really think that. What I think is that she knew the Talleys more intimately than anyone else.''

''Granted.''

''And if there's anything at all that isn't in your file, she may know it. But how am I going to find her after forty years?''

He pulled the bottom sheet of folded paper out from under the other two, folded it in half and in half again, and wrote Magda Wandowska along the top edge. "Okay," he said thoughtfully, "let's see what we know about her. In 1950 she's eighteen years old and a recent immigrant from Eastern Europe. And she's a good Catholic. Either she stayed home and took care of Mom and Pop in their old age or she married. If she married, her name's different."

"Right, but she married in the parish church. They published the banns and they'll have a record of the marriage."

"Good thinking," he said with approval. "I could run up there next week and ask around."

"No. Let's just find out where the church is. I'm very good with clergy."

He looked at me, then said, "Okay. We got that one out of the way."

"There's something else." I took a sip of my iced coffee. It was such a long shot. "The Talleys lived nicely. Mrs. Talley paid Magda a dollar an hour. When I was reading the *Times* on microfilm the other day, I looked at the want ads. Do you know that people earned fifty-seven and a half cents an hour in 1950?"

He gave me the nice smile. "I didn't."

"So a dollar an hour was a lot of money for housecleaning and baby-sitting."

"Agreed."

"And it didn't sound as though Mrs. Talley worked at all."

"Not if the Wandowska girl was the only baby-sitter."

"So what did she live on?" I watched his face.

"You're talking about the missing husband."

"Right. I saw no mention of him in any of the newspapers I read on microfilm."

"He's written up in the file."

"Really?" I had been so sure I'd made a clever discovery, "How did they find him?"

"Well, you start off making the same observations and assumptions that you did. Then you go to the local banks and find the one she keeps her money in. Once a month there's a deposit made, a check, always the same amount. From there, it's pretty easy to find the guy who wrote the checks.''

I hoped I didn't look as disappointed as I felt. ''Are his name and address in the file?''

''Sure. I'll give it to you when we get back to the house.'' He signaled the waitress. ''Dessert?'' he asked me.

''Not for me.''

He got the check and pulled out his wallet. I took mine out of my bag and glanced over at the check.

''My treat,'' he said.

''Sergeant, this is very much a business lunch, and you're the one doing me the favor.''

That seemed to amuse him. ''How's about your treat next time?''

By the time he had said it, the waitress had picked up check and bills and was on her way to the cashier.

''Thank you.''

''Let's get back to the house and look at that file.''

9

The day was beautiful, warm and dry. The intense humid heat of summer had not yet attacked the city. A slight breeze carried the scent of fruits and vegetables from a small shop as we passed.

''You a teacher?'' he asked.

''Yes. How'd you guess? Was I very schoolmarmish at lunch?''

"Nothing like that. It's June and you're not working. Just seemed the obvious thing. What do you teach?"

"English."

"Ah."

"Poetry," I said, to allay his fears. "Not grammar."

"That's good. High school?"

"College. I'll be teaching a course this fall on Poetry and the Contemporary American Woman." I laughed at my private joke.

"Sounds like fun."

"I think so, too."

"I took seven years to get a college degree while I was on the job."

I was impressed. "That must have meant lots of long days and hard nights."

"It was. But it was worth it. I think I missed the course on Poetry and the Contemporary American Woman."

I laughed again. "So did I. I wanted to spend the summer preparing for it. That was until I took on the Talley murder."

"Well, we'll see where it goes. By the way, my name is Jack."

"Hi. I'm Chris." I offered my hand and we shook. He had a nice firm grip. As I said, I like that.

"Get anything done on the course so far?" he asked.

"Just the very beginning. I thought I should start out with something very concrete, very fundamental."

"Like what?"

" 'Gather ye rosebuds while ye may,' " I quoted.

"Amen," Sergeant Jack Brooks said, opening the door to the station house.

The file for DD case number 211/50 was large, heavy, and tied with a piece of dirty old string. Although the sergeant—I hadn't yet come to think of him as Jack—had felt some reservations about the thoroughness of the investigation, it turned out to be far more complete than I had anticipated.

The most compelling part of the file was the photographs. They were black-and-white and the most gruesome things I had ever seen. Looking at them, you could almost believe the photographer had some neurotic need to show horror. There were pictures of Mrs. Talley taken from every conceivable angle, and pictures of the kitchen to show blood-stains and spatterings. The knife was photographed. Smudges of blood in the twins' room and the bathroom were photographed.

After seeing the body, you could understand the quote I had read on microfilm: "Only a madman could have done something like that." She had been slashed everywhere.

But "madman" wasn't a term I would use to describe the twins. They were retarded, but far from "mad."

"Pretty gory," Jack Brooks said at my side.

"Worse than I expected."

"In 1950 forensics was pretty much the crime scene. They took a lot of pictures and had someone do a sketch of the crime scene." He rummaged in the file. "Here it is, signed and dated." He laid it in front of me.

It was done on graph paper, but it looked like one of those diagrams of an apartment for rent, except that furniture was also sketched in, and in the kitchen section there was an outline of a body and a notation of where the knife was found. The dimensions of each room were noted. The living room was twelve by twenty, a nice-size room, and both bedrooms were generous. I made a quick sketch in my notebook and set the pictures and diagrams aside to look at the interviews.

On the basis of Magda's testimony, the police had visited Mrs. Talley's hairdresser on King's Highway. Yes, she had had a ten-thirty appointment on Good Friday, and yes, she had arrived on time. Marie Guerreira had shampooed her and set her hair in pin curls. Mrs. Talley had sat under the hair dryer for about her usual thirty minutes, reading one of the women's magazines the shop subscribed to. Marie had then combed her out. Before leaving, Mrs. Talley had wished her a Happy Easter.

There were also records of interviews with so many of the Talleys' neighbors that I was impressed in spite of myself. I went through them fairly quickly. They didn't seem to add much, partly because at least half the neighbors didn't really know who Mrs. Talley was. Almost all of them had seen the twins, but that was as far as "knowing the Talleys" went. Many of the tenants were afraid of the twins, but the officers doing the questioning didn't delve into why. The fear just seemed to add credence to the obvious, that Robert and James had knifed their mother to death.

I paused over the interview with Selma Franklin. Although the interviews were notes of conversations, not transcribed tapes or statements written by those interviewed, phrases that I had heard Mrs. Franklin say leaped off the page at me. "She would walk her children, I would walk mine." "Mrs. T: What color is the light? Green. Mrs. T: We can cross the street." It had been a very powerful memory.

What interested me most was the interview with Patrick Talley, the twins' father. Patrick Talley had carved out a whole new life for himself, separate from his wife and sons, and perhaps unknown to them. He lived in New Jersey, not far from the George Washington Bridge, in a small house "with a younger woman" named Anne Garfield, but the name on the door was Talley. Besides the "younger woman," there were also two children, Patrick Jr. and Kathleen. I felt a lot of emotion when I read that. From the ages of the children, fourteen and twelve, I figured he had left his first family before the twins were fourteen years old, possibly long before, and set up a second household without benefit of divorce or clergy. I wondered as I began the interviews with Mr. Talley and Anne whether the children knew the reality of their parents' relationship. Considering their ages and the era we were talking about, I guessed that they didn't.

Patrick Talley Sr. was an insurance salesman, and apparently quite a good one. He and his second family lived comfortably, if not sumptuously, on his earnings alone. Anne Garfield, who said she was known as Mrs. Talley, was a housewife and mother. She had her own car, she explained, because Pat needed one full-time for his business.

As for Patrick Talley's whereabouts on Good Friday, he

had had a morning appointment at a small plant in New Jersey (for which he had landed the account), which had developed into lunch. He had returned home about three—corroborated by Anne—done the paperwork required by the morning's work, and taken a nap before dinner. No one in the family went to church.

It became clear as I read that the parents were very anxious to keep all knowledge of the terrible events of Good Friday a secret from their children, strengthening my belief that they knew nothing of their father's marriage and less about his other offspring.

I wrote down the address in New Jersey with little hope of finding anyone who would remember Patrick Talley, but at least it was a starting point.

At three I took a break from my reading and found the Brooklyn phone book. I looked up both Wandowska and Wandowski but found no Magda and no one at the 1950 address. According to the file, her father's name had been Peter, and he might still be alive today, but if so, he didn't have a phone listed in his name, or he had moved. Her mother's name had been Anna, and there was no listing for her either.

"Find anything?"

I looked up. Jack Brooks was standing beside the desk I was sitting at with the directory open before me.

"Nothing."

"Try Wandowski?"

"Yes."

"Hold on. Let me ask one of the guys."

He went to an occupied desk and I heard him say something about a church in some other area of Brooklyn. When he came back, he said, "Infant of Prague. I'll write down how you get there. Sure you want to do this yourself?"

"You bet."

He wrote several lines on a sheet of paper and handed it to me folded. "How 'bout giving me your number so I can call you if I think of anything."

I gave it to him.

"Think you'll be back?"

"I'm sure of it. But first I'd like to find Magda."

He looked at his watch. "You probably ought to get going. You've got a long drive, and once you get into rush hour, everything starts overheating."

"I'll just tidy up." We went back to the desk with the Talley file and I put things in order, got a fresh piece of string, and tied up the precious package. "This detective, Kevin O'Connor," I said. "I see his name everywhere. I first noticed it in one of the newspaper articles."

"He was the guy assigned to the case. The first two cops who answered Magda's call probably walked in the apartment, saw what was up, and called for the uniform patrol sergeant. He comes over and calls the precinct detective squad. When they get there, they give the case a complaint number. That's on this UF61 form here." He showed it to me. "Then they call the Brooklyn Homicide Squad, and O'Connor's the guy who's catching cases at the time. He's probably pretty ticked off; it's Easter, and the last thing he needs is to do overtime. I'd bet he stopped for something to eat before he answered the call."

"You're joking."

"Never. A cop always thinks about where his next meal is coming from. Homicide investigations are always long and drawn-out. If you don't eat before it starts, you may not get a chance for hours. Anyway, he goes to the address and adds a homicide number to the complaint number. That's his handwriting here."

"And then he starts his investigation."

"Which lasts for hours and hours in the apartment."

"How can I find him?"

Jack Brooks took a folded sheet of paper off his desk, turned it to a clean side, and made a note. "I'll look into it."

"Thank you. Lots." I gathered my notes and my bag.

Jack Brooks walked me out of the building.

"Thank you," I said again when we were on the sidewalk.

"Can we get together some time?" he asked.

Of course, I had known it was coming, and of course, I didn't want to deal with it right now. "Sure," I said, happy that I could get the single syllable out in one piece. " 'Bye."

"So long."

I turned back halfway down the block. He was still watching me and I waved. When I got home, I marched into the bathroom, stood in front of the medicine chest, and stared at my face in the mirror.

10

I'm not bad-looking. My hair is kind of a nice shade of brown, still pretty short because of the habit I wore. I'd been blowing it dry without benefit of mirror, but it seemed to do the right thing naturally, which is certainly a plus. My face is fine. It's got the usual number of eyes and nose, and put together, I'd say it's not unpleasing. How's that for modesty?

You understand I have never had a relationship with a man. I've met men who were attractive to me and some who found me attractive. But let me set the record straight: I didn't leave St. Stephen's because I had formed a relationship with a man or because I wanted to. Nor did I leave because I had uncontrollable urges. I left because I felt I had accomplished all I could as a nun. I wanted to do more with my life, and I needed to be outside the convent to achieve anything new.

From the time my leaving the convent started to look like a possibility, I thought about marrying and having children. I wasn't sure how it would happen, but I felt that the smart thing would be to move slowly. I scarcely imagined that less than a month after I moved to Oakwood, I would meet an attractive man who would want to take me out. It was a little

unnerving. But it goes without saying it made me feel warm
and happy and started certain formerly repressed emotions
working.

The phone rang before nine on Saturday morning.

"This is Virginia McAlpin. I hope it isn't too early to
telephone?"

"Not at all." I had already walked and breakfasted.

"I've been in touch with Dr. Sanderson. He's my contact
at New Hope. Do you think you might be able to see him on
Monday? I tried to call several times yesterday, but you
weren't home."

"I spent most of the day at a police station in Brooklyn."

"Good heavens." She sounded shocked. "I hope nothing's wrong."

"I was reading the file on the Talley murder, Mrs. Mc-
Alpin."

"Oh my, you really are humming along."

I didn't feel like recounting what I'd done, especially
because I had nothing substantive to report, so I ignored her
leading comment. "I'd like very much to see Dr. Sanderson
on Monday. Where exactly is New Hope located?"

"Up near Albany, but not that far. You could go up to 287
and cut west to Route 9. That's the scenic route. Or you could
take—"

I knew Route 9 like the back of my hand. It was the road
to St. Stephen's. "Fine," I said. "I know the area. It
shouldn't take more than two hours."

"Less," Mrs. McAlpin said. "Dr. Sanderson drives it
himself frequently."

I wrote down his name, Elmont Sanderson, and directions
to the hospital. Mrs. McAlpin said she would confirm our
11:00 A.M. appointment.

Then I drove to Brooklyn to find the Church of the Infant
of Prague.

It was large and old and stone, the way I like churches to
be. I walked in through the great front doors to admire the

interior. Then I lit three candles, one each for my father, mother, and Aunt Meg. I can't tell you I have any belief connected with that, but it's the sort of thing they would want me to do, and I do it whenever I enter a church.

I found the office and went inside. A middle-aged woman sat at the desk.

I said, "Good morning," and she looked up.

She smiled as if she meant it. "How can I help you?"

"I'm trying to find someone who was probably married in this church about thirty-five years ago. Maybe a little more."

"May I ask you why?"

"Someone she knew was murdered in 1950. I need to talk to her about it. I think she would want to speak to me. She felt the people charged with the murder didn't do it. I feel the same way."

"Just a moment." She pushed herself away from the desk. "Let me see if Father is free."

I hoped he would be. Every Catholic church keeps records of the banns of matrimony, and it's a simple thing to look up a name if you have some idea of the time frame. Girls usually marry in their parish church. If Magda had married, this was the place that would have the records.

The secretary returned. "Father Olshansky will see you now," she said formally.

"Thank you." I went through the door, and she pulled it shut behind me.

Father Olshansky was not young, but he wasn't old enough to have been here in 1950. "I understand you're looking for a parishioner," he said, folding his hands on the desk in front of him.

"Her name was Magda Wandowska," I said, and gave him a little background.

He didn't seem familiar with the Talley murder, but he was pleased that I was working on behalf of the sons. "Let's check the banns," he said. "What year would that have been?"

"I don't really know," I admitted. "But it must have been after April 1950."

"Good enough." He went to his file, and I watched him move quickly through the cards.

She must have married, I thought, wondering what I would do if Father Olshansky failed to find her name.

"Well, here we are," he said. "June of 1952. Magda Wandowska and Richard Zygowsky."

I was scribbling as he spoke. He spelled the name and I printed it carefully. "Wonderful," I breathed.

"Now let's look at the current census and see if they're still in the parish." He tried another file but failed to find the name. "They may have moved, of course, but they would have come to us for baptism records and the like. Let's see if they had any children while they still lived here."

It was plain he enjoyed detecting, and I was happy to have him enjoy himself.

"Well, there we are, a boy, named after his father, born in 1954. That would make him about thirty-six now, wouldn't you think?"

"Yes, indeed. You deserve a medal, Father."

"But we haven't found her yet, have we? Let's see if Mrs. Zygowsky was a faithful member of the Legion of Mary." He went on with his poking through records. "Aha. She certainly was. And moved away in 1965."

"Would you happen to know where?" At this point, I was holding my breath.

"It looks as though Father Thomascevich wrote a letter to the new parish and forwarded the records. They moved to Queens." He called off the address and I wrote it in my book.

I put my book back in my bag and took out my wallet. "I'd like to leave a gift for the church, Father. Do you have a box for St. Anthony?" St. Anthony, if you're not up on your saints, helps people to find things.

"You'll find it near the front door."

"Thank you very much."

"And thank you, Sister."

I had turned toward the door when I heard the word. "How did you know?" I asked, turning back.

"Oh, the hair mostly. Looks chopped up, the way the nuns have it who wear a habit. Have you given up the habit or given up the convent?"

"I left the convent," I said, feeling just a little guilty for the first time.

"I'm sorry. We lose so many of our best. Well, good luck in your search."

I found a stationery store about a block from the church and bought one of those Hagstrom's maps of Queens. Then I went into a phone booth and called information.

The Zygowskys lived at the address the priest had given me. I dialed the number.

"Hello?" It was sort of a pinched voice.

"Mrs. Zygowsky?"

"Yes?"

"Magda Zygowsky?"

"Who is this?"

"My name is Christine Bennett, Mrs. Zygowsky. A few days ago I met James Talley."

"Omigod," the voice said faintly. Then, "You saw James? How is he? How is Robert? Oh, my poor boys."

"James is fine, Mrs. Zygowsky. I haven't seen Robert. I'd like to speak to you if I could. I'm looking into the murder of Mrs. Talley. I'm hoping to prove the twins didn't do it."

"Oh, God bless you. This afternoon? Can you come today?"

"How's two o'clock?"

"Yes, two. Let me see, the bakery is open."

More tea and cookies, I thought, wondering how many pounds the Talley murder would put on me. "You don't have to feed me, Mrs. Zygowsky," I said. "I just want to—"

"Yes, yes, just come. Take the Long Island Expressway."

"I'll be there."

* * *

If you've never tried to find your way around Queens, you still have a challenging experience ahead of you. Roads, drives, avenues, and courts all have the same name, and to make matters worse, the names are numbers. Just because you've come to Sixty-ninth Drive, don't be deluded into thinking that Seventieth Drive is at the next intersection. You may not reach it for hours, or so it seemed to me. But I found the Zygowskys' two-family house with time to spare.

I managed to cross from Brooklyn into Queens without requiring a bridge or a tunnel or even the Long Island Expressway, and then I worked my way toward the area on the map that was labeled Maspeth. I had never heard of it, but it was near Forest Hills, which I had heard of. Then I drove through streets and roads and avenues until I reached the Zygowskys' address. Parking, as usual, was a near impossible feat, but I just kept circling the area till someone piled his family into a car and pulled out for a Saturday afternoon excursion.

Magda Zygowsky came down from the second-floor apartment calling, "Hello," as she descended.

"Mrs. Zygowsky?" I said as the door opened.

She smiled, her face bright and open. "Please come in."

"Hi. Glad to meet you. I'm Christine Bennett."

We went up the stairs into a comfortable living room where the wood gleamed and I was sure I smelled furniture polish.

"Make yourself comfortable. The tea is almost ready. You drink tea?"

"Yes, thank you."

She still spoke with that slight Slavic flavor that indicated her origin. "Tell me," she said, leaning forward eagerly. "Tell me about the boys."

She had fair skin and light hair and eyes. The hair was graying the way it does sometimes with blondes; it just seems to creep over from gold to gray by degrees so that you're never sure when it has crossed the line. She had it cut short, and of course, she was a woman in her late fifties, but she was clearly Magda.

"James is in a group home now," I began. I went on to

tell her what little I knew of his past. "He's very quiet now," I said at the end. "He asks for his brother."

"And the brother? Where is Robert?"

"I don't know that."

"They kept them apart." I felt sure she wanted to add, "the bastards," but she couldn't. "They only had each other, you know?"

"I know."

"And you think they didn't do it?"

"I don't know, but I hope so. I'm trying to find as many people as I can to question. Infant of Prague in Brooklyn found you for me. On Monday I'm going to talk to a psychiatrist at the institution where they kept James until recently."

"Wait. I bring you the tea."

The tea was accompanied by a tray of rich pastries. I waited till the tea had been poured and Magda had encouraged me to select and dig into something from the tray. Then I went on.

"Mrs. Zygowsky, you were the one who found Mrs. Talley. Can you go over it with me, tell me exactly what happened? You still remember it, don't you?"

"Like it happened this morning, I remember it." Her face clouded. Then she leaned forward again and put her hand over mine. "You call me Magda, okay? I am Magda, you are Christine."

"Thank you, Magda." I was glad she had suggested it since it was the way I thought of her.

She sat back in her chair and went through it all again, starting with the morning of Good Friday, skipping Saturday, and then, after a deep breath, how she pushed the doorbell and let herself in. She remembered everything in wonderful detail, the color of the living room rug, where the furniture was placed—she got up and showed me in her own living room: "The sofa was just so against the wall, and here, by the window, she had one of those big plants you find in the desert." I felt myself walking through the apartment with her in her fear of finding Mrs. Talley fallen in the bathroom or sick in her bedroom. My stomach did funny things as we came, finally, to the kitchen.

She stopped, pulled a tissue from her dress pocket, and held it in her hand, as though afraid she would cry. "It was terrible. It was the most terrible thing you ever see."

"I can imagine. I read the accounts in the paper, and it sounded to me that you were really very brave, considering how young you were."

"I had no choice, Christine," she said. "Somebody had to take care of those boys, you know?"

"Weren't you afraid, even a little, that they had done it?"

"Later maybe, later when the police said it couldn't have been anyone else, I thought maybe. But at that moment I thought, someone has come in and murdered this wonderful woman."

"Why did you think she was wonderful?"

"She was good to me. She was a good person. She lived without a husband and she took care of the boys. She was always patient with them. I don't think it was so easy."

I agreed with her on that. "Did anyone ever come to the apartment while you were there?" I asked.

She looked thoughtful for a moment. "I think nobody. Maybe the super. Maybe something from the drugstore. No, I am wrong. Once the doctor came, just as I was leaving."

"The doctor? Was someone sick?"

"For the boys. You know, the psychiatrist." She stumbled a bit over the word. The Zygowskys had lived without benefit of shrinks. "He studied them, you know? He asked them questions. They could remember anything, those boys."

"I heard about it. You wouldn't remember his name, would you?"

Magda smiled and shook her head. "It's so long, so long. He was an older man, a little gray. He carried a leather briefcase and he wore those leather patches here." She placed a hand on her opposite elbow.

"He only came once?" I asked.

"Only once when I was there. But I know he came other times. The boys told me. He would ask them, what happened this time, what happened that time? He played the radio for them sometimes, and the boys could tell him back every word.'' She laughed. "Like a record. They were so clever.''

"Magda, the police said nothing was stolen from the apartment. What do you think?''

"How could I know? I cleaned Mrs. Talley's bedroom, but I never opened her drawer. If something was gone, how would I know? The apartment looked the same to me. There was blood, but that was because the boys touched their mama and got blood on their hands. But I think everything was there. Did they find her pocketbook?''

"I don't know, but I'm sure it's in the police file. If it had been missing, they would certainly have looked for a thief.''

"Sure. You're right. Sure it was there.'' She sipped her tea. "You know, I trusted her so much, I came from my home with only one subway fare. I knew she would give me for coming on Easter. I had to ask the policeman for my fare. They drove me home.''

"They were kind to you, weren't they?''

"Very kind. Very good people.''

"It said in the papers that you took one of the twins and put him in Mrs. Talley's bedroom. Why did you do that?''

"Just to keep them quiet so I could think. Sometimes they would talk, talk, talk when they were together, like the radio. And that day they were crying, 'Mama, Mama.' Such a terrible thing. You should never live through anything like it.''

"Magda, who do you think killed Mrs. Talley?''

"Somebody. A stranger.''

"A neighbor who didn't like her?''

"I don't think so. Today maybe, not then. Then we were more friends. Today we are more enemies.''

"Did she have any problems with the neighbors?'' I asked, not very hopeful of receiving a useful reply.

"Oh, I don't think so,'' Magda said quickly. "Well, maybe just the one downstairs.''

"Who was that?''

"Some lady who banged on the ceiling when anybody walked on the floor. Mrs. Talley would laugh at it, but sometimes it gave her a headache. We didn't make noise, Christine. But some people have those carpets that go everywhere, and they think the rest of us should do that, too."

I decided to check, wondering how angry a woman might become from hearing footsteps overhead. Angry enough to kill? But then, that was New York, and New Yorkers were known to be strange people.

I glanced at my notes. There was probably nothing new here, except for the description of the Talley apartment, but I was still hopeful. "Did you ever see the twins again?" I asked.

She shook her head and looked sorrowful. Finally she said, "I asked the police where they were and I sent them Christmas cards. Once or twice I called the hospital and asked about them. I always said, 'Tell him Magda called,' but you never know, do you? Not like today, everybody calls all over the country and it costs nothing. But I never saw them."

"James is very gray," I said. "He sits by himself most of the time. But he's in a good place now, a real home. It's not a criminal institution."

"That's good. And where is Robert?"

"I don't know. I'm trying to find out."

"Maybe I go and say hello one day."

"That would be very nice of you, Magda."

"You think they did it, Christine?"

"I still don't know."

"Listen to me, they didn't. They were good boys, you know? They loved their Mama. They were *crying* when I came in. But who did it?" she asked rhetorically, and shook her head. "I donno, I donno."

I got up to leave and remembered something else. "Did anyone ever telephone while you were there?" I asked, feeling rather foolish, asking someone to remember if a phone had rung forty years ago.

But Magda took it seriously, as she had all my questions. "There was a phone, yes. I called her, she called me. Sometimes she talked to a friend. Maybe it rang when I was there."

I thanked her for her time, her information, her hospitality. Then I wrote my name and phone number on one of my sheets and tore it out. "If you think of anything, please call. Call collect," I said, to encourage her.

She said she would and she smiled, almost for the first time. I had brought back a lot of unhappy memories.

As I drove home, sorting my way through the streets of Queens, I felt sorry that I had ever thought that she was a suspect.

11

The Monday appointment with Dr. Sanderson was for eleven in the morning. I left home at nine to give myself plenty of time, and let the car drive itself toward St. Stephen's. As Virginia McAlpin had suggested, I crossed Westchester County on Route 287 and then turned north on Route 9, which stayed on the east side of the Hudson River up to Albany. Across the Hudson the Thruway zipped along, but I always preferred the older, somewhat slower, more picturesque road I had chosen. After Poughkeepsie, I felt familiar stirrings. St. Stephen's was not far. In the past, I had gotten off Route 9 south of the convent and worked my way up and over on local roads. This was my first time driving north of it, and I wondered if I would see a spire as I passed. Maybe, I thought, smiling at the possibility, that was the vantage point that gave you the legendary view of the Hudson.

But I could see nothing identifiable, and finally I knew I had passed the last point at which I might have been able to see it.

* * *

I arrived at New Hope long before my appointment, and
I spent some time walking through the nearby town. When
I turned in to the parking lot and saw the dismal prisonlike
building with its barred windows, I felt a surge of pity for
the quiet, sad man who had spent forty years of what passed
for life here.

Dr. Sanderson took me on time, shook my hand, and sat,
not behind his desk, but in a chair matching the one he had
offered me. He was probably in his early forties, again far
too young to have known James very long.

"Virginia McAlpin has explained your interest in James
Talley. I've reviewed his records this morning, and I can tell
you that I knew him personally in the years I've been here.
What would you like to ask me?"

"The big question is whether you think he may have been
innocent of the murder of his mother."

Dr. Sanderson smiled in a way that made me feel I had
asked a naive question. I don't relate well to psychiatrists.
They make me uncomfortable. "It's very possible that James
is innocent," he said. "It's also possible that he's guilty. I
would like to be able to tell you that I succeeded where all
my predecessors failed, that is, in getting inside him. No one
seems to have done that in all the years that he was here, and
an amazing number of professionals seem to have tried.
There's a great fascination with savants."

"I'm sure there is."

"But the record shows a slow but constant deterioration
in his abilities. When he entered New Hope he was able to
dress himself, tie his shoelaces, hang up his clothes, select
his food, participate in certain activities. None of that is true
anymore. He needs a great deal of attention."

"Perhaps," I suggested, "that's due to a kind of leth-
argy."

"I couldn't discount that."

"And depression," I added. "He still asks for his
brother."

"That is also possible. It wouldn't be the first time that has occurred."

"Can you tell me why he was separated from his brother when they were all the family each one had?"

"A recommendation was made to the court in 1950," Dr. Sanderson said. "By a psychiatrist, most likely, or perhaps also by a social worker or psychologist. The judge usually follows those recommendations. It was actually done, whether you find this credible or not, to help the brothers develop independently."

"Do you know whether his brother has developed better than James?"

"In fact, I do. His behavior has pretty much mirrored James's, with the exception of a few small points. A study was done just a few years ago of the twins and published in a journal."

"I'd like to read that."

"I'll have a copy made for you."

"Thank you. I understand that before the murder, the twins were the subject of a great deal of study. A psychiatrist came to the apartment sometimes to conduct experiments."

"That would be Dr. Weintraub. I believe he died in the early eighties. I have his published papers, too, if you're interested."

"Very much."

"They're quite fascinating. Dr. Weintraub recounts one visit where one of the twins started delivering a speech of remarkable scope and sophistication. It turned out to be a speech President Truman had given and which Mrs. Talley had listened to on the radio. There were many other feats they performed, determining in a couple of seconds how many straws Mrs. Talley had dropped on the floor, recalling what happened on days they had lived through, putting a day on any date you gave them using the current calendar."

I had heard much of this from Mrs. McAlpin, but hearing it again simply added to the wonder. "Do you have an opinion on why they lost those abilities?"

Dr. Sanderson smiled. "I have lots of opinions," he said,

and I started to like him. "The shock of realizing what they had done after they killed their mother or, alternatively, the shock of seeing someone murder her. You can take your choice. The police and the courts seemed convinced of the former. Are you convinced of the alternative?"

"I'm not," I admitted. "And it could be I'm grasping at straws. I think what I'm looking for is some small indication that they might not have done it. This Dr. Weintraub, did he have an opinion?"

"He had a very strong one. He believed they could not have done it."

I felt a small flutter of elation. "Did he say it publicly or publish it anywhere?"

"It was published in a letter somewhere. I'll have to dig it up. Quite a famous letter, as I recall."

"But the courts chose to ignore him?"

"He wasn't called to testify. The prosecutor called his own psychiatrist."

"And the defense? The twins must have been represented by counsel."

"I believe they were, but I don't know the details."

"Do you know where Robert is now, Dr. Sanderson?"

"He was also permitted to leave a high-security institution when his brother did. He's in a group home, similar to Greenwillow, near Buffalo. I've been in touch with the director, and his behavior seems to be quite similar to James's, as it has been since the murder."

"Do you think the decision to separate them was correct?"

"It was correct for several reasons. Besides affording the opportunity for the twins to develop independently, there's a strong possibility that together they might be capable of murder while separately they might not. It may have taken a certain courage, a certain companionship if you will, to commit the act, which neither twin possessed alone. If you want my opinion on whether James Talley is capable of murder today, I will answer unhesitatingly no. If they're together, I can't give you an opinion."

"You think they may be dangerous together?"

"Frankly, I don't, but I don't discount the possibility."

"Would you have any objections to getting them together?"

The doctor pursed his lips, then said, "At this point, I can't say I would. It might be interesting to see whether they remember each other."

"Let me set some facts out before you as I see them," I said, trying to make some sense out of the bits and pieces that seemed to have no structure. "On the morning of Good Friday, Magda, the girl who came to the house three mornings a week, took the twins out for a walk, and they performed one of their marvelous mental feats for her. They recalled the day she was born eighteen years earlier, when they were only eleven. She found it very remarkable, and she told the police about it when they questioned her on Easter Sunday.

"But on Easter Sunday they had lost their gift. The police questioned them for hours, first at the apartment and then later at the police station. I'm sure the police threatened them. There was no Miranda warning forty years ago, and they didn't get a lawyer right away. But even with all that pressure, they didn't say anything. They could have blamed each other, but they didn't. They could have broken down and confessed. They could have blamed some other person. None of that happened. Can you account for that in any way, Doctor?"

"Not in any way that will satisfy you. All I can say is the obvious, that between the morning of Good Friday and the morning of Easter Sunday, something very profound happened to change those two young men. In a very real sense, the twins that performed for Magda on Good Friday were not the same people who were arrested on Easter Sunday."

"Do you think, if James knows who did the killing, that he has the mental competence to keep it a secret?"

"That's the most puzzling aspect of the whole case, Miss Bennett. Keeping a secret requires rather sophisticated thinking. I don't think he has it. Dr. Weintraub didn't think he had it. Still, forty years have passed and he's said nothing."

"Maybe he was locked in a bedroom while it happened."

"Possibly. But he would know who locked him up, wouldn't he?" He smiled. "It's a tough one."

"Who arranged for James to go to Greenwillow?" I asked.

"The court did, with my recommendation."

The surprise must have shown on my face. "You," I said.

"As I told you earlier, I don't think James is capable of murder. I'm also less than wholehearted about punitive detention. And he's been incarcerated longer than most people convicted in the state of New York—without having ever been convicted. In my small way, I'm something of a civil libertarian." He looked at his watch. "Shall we have a bite to eat in the village? It's past twelve."

"I'd like that."

We ate in a coffee shop with good home cooking and spent an hour or more talking. I told him I had recently left St. Stephen's and he seemed very interested in that, in why I had entered and why I had left. He was a kind man with a great capacity for empathy. When he told me about his family, I felt honored, as though perhaps he felt that I, too, had some of the qualities needed to listen and respond. In the short time I knew him, I altered some of my feelings about the profession and especially about its practitioners.

When we returned to New Hope, it was nearly two. Dr. Sanderson picked up the address of Robert Talley's group home and promised to have his secretary send me copies of all the relevant articles he had mentioned as soon as they could be unearthed.

Then we shook hands and I drove away.

It was a beautiful day and I drove south at a leisurely speed. When I approached the turnoff for St. Stephen's, I began to feel a compelling tug. I wanted to see it again, to see the people I had left behind. Something in me craved a look at the grounds, which were surely the most beautiful I would ever see, the somewhat dank scent of the chapel, the sight of nuns hurrying along the paths. I had not left in anger as many nuns do nowadays, or because a relationship with a man had caused me to turn against my vows. I had left because I had decided over a long period of time that it would be better for me and therefore ultimately better for the convent. I had departed with a lot of goodwill, leaving behind friends. Today I wanted to see them.

"Too soon, Kix," I said aloud, and hearing my voice, I knew it was true. I needed to establish myself in my new community and do this job that I had promised to do before I went back to say hello.

I drove past the turnoff and kept driving south, finally, some time later, stopping in Poughkeepsie. I had never seen Vassar, and here was the perfect day to do it.

After my visit, I had dinner in town and set out for home. It was after eight when I entered Oakwood and slowed down to drive through the familiar streets, looking out for young baseball players and skateboarders as I neared Pine Brook Road.

Although my life has had its share of drama, I usually look with suspicion at breathlessly described dramatic moments so beloved by writers. But what happened that evening as I returned from New Hope surely had all the elements of high drama.

It was dusk as I turned in to my driveway. The automatic timers Aunt Meg had set before her final illness had turned on three lights in the house, giving it a comfortable, lived-in look. I drove into the garage, pulled the door down, and walked to the back door. The garage is detached from the house, something Aunt Meg always considered a plus. ("It doesn't look like one of those boxes the builders throw up all over town.") As I turned the key, I heard the phone ringing.

For the first three weeks that I lived in the house, the phone rang so infrequently that it startled me when I heard it. The last few days, of course, had brought a change, and there were so many people who might be calling me with information I could scarcely wait to hear that I pushed the door open, leaving my key in the lock, dropped my bag as I ran

to the kitchen, and answered with a breathless "Hello?" on
what must have been the fifth or sixth ring.

"Hello? Christine? It's you?" the somewhat high-pitched
voice with its still audible relic of Eastern Europe said in my
ear.

"Magda? Yes, it's me. What is it?"

"Christine, I am so glad to reach you. How are you?"

I've never been very good on the telephone. I have used it
almost exclusively to get information and conduct business.
People who start conversations with polite, meaningless ex-
changes tend to drive me crazy, but I've learned to play the
game.

"Fine," I said conversationally, not asking how she was
in return.

"I've tried you all evening, but you weren't home."

"I've been out all day. I just got in."

"Well, that's good. I thought maybe I wrote down the
number wrong."

Please, I thought, please tell me. "It was the right number. Did you think of something to tell me?"

"Something small but maybe important, you know?"

"What is it?" I struggled not to sound impatient.

"I thought of it after you left, and I didn't know if I should
bother to call."

"Of course you should call. What was it, Magda?"

"When the police were ready to take the boys away that
night, I couldn't find Robert's coat."

"It was missing?"

"It wasn't in the closet. James's coat was there, and both
raincoats. Each boy had a nice, warm dark winter coat and
a raincoat. Mrs. Talley had her fur coat there, a Persian lamb,
a beautiful coat, you know? And her wool coat and her spring
coat. That was about all. But when it was time for the boys
to be taken away, Robert's coat wasn't in the closet."

"Did you look for it, Magda?"

"Oh yes. I was there the whole day. I didn't have carfare
and I was afraid to ask. And since the boys knew me, I would

sit with one and then the other while the police questioned them, to keep them calm and quiet, you know?''

"Yes, I understand. And when it came time to leave?''

"I went to the closet and looked for their coats.''

"And one coat wasn't there,'' I prompted.

"Robert's coat. They had the same coats, and Mrs. Talley had put a piece of tape in the coats with their name in big letters. Robert knew to read his name, and James knew to read his.''

"Is there anywhere else the coats could have been?''

"Nowhere. Mrs. Talley put everything in its place. When I came home with the boys on Good Friday, I hung the coats in the closet.''

"And if Mrs. Talley died on Friday, probably they hadn't been out since.''

"That is what I think. There is one more thing.''

The news had gotten me very excited. "Yes,'' I said.

"When I opened the closet, there was a big hole in between the coats.''

"A hole?''

"Like maybe someone went push, push, push till he found what he was looking for. You know what I mean?''

"Yes, I do. As if he was looking for a man's coat to put on.''

"Yes, to cover up the blood on his shirt.''

"And when he found it, he left the 'hole' between the coats.''

"Yes!'' Magda sounded pleased that I was following her story.

"Magda, did you tell anyone about the missing coat?''

"When I couldn't find Robert's coat, I told that policeman—I forget his name now.''

"O'Connor?'' I suggested hesitantly.

"Yes! O'Connor! That was the name. A good-looking young man, he was, with blue eyes. I said, 'Robert's coat is not in the closet,' and he said, 'Find something else. It's seven o'clock and it's Easter Sunday. I must get home.' ''

I could hear the young, handsome detective saying it in his

own words: "Look, it's seven o'clock on Easter Sunday and I gotta get home. Just find something for him to put on, will ya?"

"What did you do, Magda?" I asked.

"I gave Robert his raincoat. Christine, I have my scrapbook in front of me. I have the picture from the newspaper of the boys coming out of the apartment house. Even in the dark, you can see one has a dark coat and one has a light one."

"You can see it in the picture?"

"I am looking at it now."

"Magda, this is really very exciting news," I said. Then something struck me. "But how is it that you didn't mention the missing coat to the reporters when you were interviewed for the newspapers?"

She made a little *mmm* sound and then said nothing. "I think . . ." she said hesitantly, but didn't go on. "Oh yes, now I remember. In the afternoon, when the policemen were finished asking me questions, I went outside the apartment for a little while. It really smelled awful in there, you know? And in the hall there were some newspaper people. I remember one man had a smelly cigar that made me cough. That's when I gave the interviews. Later, when we were ready to go, is when I found the coat missing."

It sounded right to me. The reporters needed that story for the Monday morning papers. "I have one more question. Did you let it go that way or did you ever report it to the police?"

"Well, when I got home, I forgot all about it. I had so much to tell my parents. But the next day, I remembered and I told my mother. I told her maybe it meant that a man had killed Mrs. Talley and stolen Robert's coat."

"Yes," I said, encouraging her.

"And my mother, God rest her soul, she said, 'Call that policeman and tell him.' "

"And did you?"

"I called the police station and asked for Detective O'Connor. But he wasn't there. So I left a message. I said one coat was missing from the apartment and maybe some-one had taken it."

"Did Detective O'Connor call you back?"

"Never." It sounded very final.

"I don't suppose you remember who you told." I threw it out, knowing there was no chance.

"No." She sounded thoughtful. "I talked to one, then another. It's so long . . . It was a funny name, you know?"

She remembered something. I almost crossed my fingers. "Yes," I said, encouraging her again.

"Like a fruit."

"A fruit?" I echoed. "You mean like apple or pear or plum?"

"Something else. I don't know. It's too long to remember such a little thing."

"Magda, I'm going to check the file and see if it's men-tioned anywhere. This is really very important. Thank you so much for calling."

"God bless you, Christine," Magda said.

I said my good-byes and hung up, my heart beating as though I had been running. It was real and it was tangible. Someone had pushed the coats aside, looking for something he could put on to cover his bloody clothes. Someone else had killed Mrs. Talley. I had it now, the physical evidence— or lack of it—that I had been searching for. There had been a killer, and he had gotten away with it for forty years.

But today his luck had run out.

12

I awoke with the kind of exuberance one needs to get moving early. But that left me with five hours before ten o'clock, Jack Brooks's starting time at work, the earliest I could call him. I ran, meeting Melanie and thanking her for Sunday dinner—she had called and invited me over, and I had gone and loved it—and then I came back, dressed, ate, and sat down at the dining room table to look over my notes.

I had to find out which apartment on the fifth floor the Talley's had lived in and see who had lived beneath them, whether that woman might still be alive, whether she would have a different opinion of the Talleys from the fairly benign ones I had heard. Then I had to figure out what to do about locating Patrick Talley's family. I had some ideas about that, and perhaps I would begin after talking to Jack Brooks.

At eight-thirty the phone rang.

"Hello?" I answered, wondering who would be calling so early.

"Hi, it's Jack. I didn't get you up, did I?"

"Been up since five, did my exercise and had my breakfast. What are you doing at work before nine?"

"I'm calling from home. I wanted to get you before you left. Tried you yesterday, but you were out."

"I went up to New Hope and spent some time talking to the psychiatrist who got James Talley into the group home."

"You're really moving." He sounded impressed, and that made me feel pretty good.

"Jack, I found out something very exciting last night. Magda called back."

"You found her?"

"On Saturday. Infant of Prague paid off. She didn't have much that was new when I saw her, but last night she did. When the police were ready to take the twins into custody, she went to the closet for their coats, and Robert's coat was missing."

"She look anywhere else?"

"She says Mrs. Talley was tidy and methodical. Also, Magda was probably the last person to bring the boys back to the apartment. They'd been out on Good Friday morning— and *she hung up their coats herself* when they got back." I said it with emphasis. "The coats were there when she left the apartment."

"You think someone put it on and walked out."

"I do."

"Because his clothes were bloody."

"Yes."

He made a little whistling sound. "You could be right."

"There's more. She told O'Connor, but he kind of waved it off. Said it was Easter Sunday and he was in a rush."

"Hungry," Jack Brooks said.

I laughed. "I know. Cops always think of their stomachs first. She called the precinct the next day and told someone about the missing coat."

"Not O'Connor."

"He wasn't there."

"So that's lost."

"Maybe not." I was surprised at my own enthusiasm and optimism. "She remembers that she left the message with someone who had a name like a fruit."

"A fruit?"

"That's what she says."

"I never heard of anyone named Joe Peach."

"Well, maybe something will occur to one of us."

"You know, there was a guy named Applebaum here a couple of years ago. I think his father was on the job. Let me look into it."

"Applebaum," I echoed. "I hadn't thought of anything like that."

"Well, it sounds like you've been busy. I've got something for you, too. I found O'Connor."

"You did!" I was ready to jump for joy.

"Retired and lives in Valley Stream, Long Island. I've got his number here."

"Shoot."

I wrote it down, glancing at my watch to see if I could decently call. I couldn't. It wasn't nine yet.

"I've talked to him myself so he'll be expecting to hear from you. Sounds like a boring old guy who sits and watches TV all day. You know where Valley Stream is?"

"Roughly."

"You can take the Throgs Neck Bridge and get on the Cross Island. Shouldn't take you too long. He can probably give you directions if he can tear himself away from the screen."

"I'll call in a little while. When you get to work, could you look up the Talleys' apartment number? Magda says there was a problem with the people downstairs."

"Will do. But I don't want you ringing doorbells."

"I've already done it."

"Chris, this is New York. It's full of crazies."

"I've just talked to a couple of people who remember the day of the murder. A little old lady in the apartment house and a man across the street, both in their eighties. The man remembers coming home from church and seeing all those blue-and-white police cars."

"They weren't blue and white."

"What?"

"Not in 1950. They were green and white. Either he doesn't remember or his memory's gone."

"He was so sure," I said. "I wrote it down just the way he said it." *The whole side of the street was filled with blue-and-white police cars.*

"Sorry."

"I'd better go back," I said.

"Call O'Connor first. But go easy. This was his case, and he *knows* he handled it right."

"I'm all tact."

"I'll get back to you with the Talleys' apartment number."

Kevin O'Connor's wife answered when I called. Her husband was out playing golf but should be back by ten or ten-thirty. He liked to play early, before it got too hot.

I got in the car and drove over to Greenwillow. James was out in the garden, presumably pulling weeds and picking up litter. I went out back and stood near the building, watching him. He looked lost, as though someone hadn't given him thorough enough instructions about what to do. He was in his shirt-sleeves, looking down at the ground, not moving. From where I stood, I couldn't tell what he was looking at, if anything.

I felt an immense wave of sorrow. Here was a man who, although retarded, had once possessed gifts so remarkable that he was the subject of study and the object of wonder. Now he had lost everything—his brother, his mother, his gifts, even the simple skills he had mastered as a child.

I walked over to him. As I approached, I saw a small piece of litter in front of him, perhaps a gum wrapper.

"Good morning, James," I said.

He looked up without recognition.

"I'm Chris. We've met before. You're James, aren't you?"

He nodded.

"Let me help you." I bent and picked up the piece of paper. James was holding a small, green plastic bag. "It goes in here, doesn't it?"

He nodded again. "My name is James."

"Yes, I know." I put the paper in his bag. "There's another piece of litter. Why don't you pick it up?"

He looked at the ground, then bent, picked up the paper, and put it in the bag.

"We make a good team," I said. "There's some more."

As we walked, I said, "James, do you remember Magda?"

He said, "Magda," and looked at me penetratingly.

"I saw Magda a few days ago. She remembers you. She thinks of you."

"Magda. See Magda."

"I saw her, yes. I think she'll come to visit you."

His face looked fearful. His eyebrows, which were thick and dense, came together as his face contracted. "Magda," he said again. "Do you know where my brother is?"

"Yes, I do, James. I do know where he is. He's fine. He asks for you."

"My brother."

"Your brother, Robert."

He seemed to tremble. I put my hand on his shoulder. "Everything's all right," I said. "Come, let's clean up some more."

I spent some time with Gene afterward, then reported to Virginia McAlpin on my visit to New Hope. When we had finished talking, it was ten-thirty and Mrs. McAlpin offered her telephone so that I could call Kevin O'Connor. He had just come home and he thought one o'clock would be a good time for us to meet. He remembered the Talley murder pretty well, he told me, but he wasn't sure he could add to the material in the file. I said I'd be there at one, and he gave me directions.

I went home to kill the intervening time and have a light, early lunch. Just as I was sitting down to a salad and iced coffee, Jack Brooks called.

"Got that apartment number for you," he said. "The Talleys lived in 5C."

"Could you hold on a moment?" I asked.

"Sure."

I put the phone down and went into the dining room. My papers were spread out and I was able to put my hand on the interview with Selma Franklin very quickly. My insides did something strange as I picked up the open notebook.

"Jack, are you sure?" I asked, getting back to the phone.

"Sure I'm sure. It's right here in front of me."

"The woman I interviewed, Selma Franklin, the one who was so sympathetic, who seemed to like Mrs. Talley and have such warm feelings toward the twins, she lived in the apartment underneath 5C. She's the one Magda said Mrs. Talley didn't get along with."

"Happens."

"But she was so good to children, so—I don't know, maybe I'm just not very good at this."

"You're damned good. You found Magda, you talked to the psychiatrist, you're going to see O'Connor. Just remember, people lie. People lie for reasons you can't guess. You ask a question and it opens up a part of their life you don't know about and they have to protect it. Maybe this Franklin woman was having an affair with Mr. Talley."

I laughed. "Not likely."

"Maybe not, but stranger things have happened. Anyway, I doubt whether a woman killed Mrs. Talley."

"Me, too." I glanced at my watch. "Thanks, Jack. I'll call you after I talk to Kevin O'Connor."

"Not so fast. Can I see you sometime? Like socially?"

"Sure," I said a little weakly.

"You say 'sure,' but you don't sound it."

"I'd like to," I said. I really wanted to, but I was feeling panicky at the prospect.

"Maybe dinner. I know a nice place up that way."

"I'd like that very much."

"Saturday."

"Saturday."

"Good."

"I'll call you later."

"I'll be here."

I hung up and went back to lunch.

13

Driving to Valley Stream, I reflected on my behavior, on the phone and off, with Jack Brooks. I sounded like two different people. On the phone I was confident as we were distant; in person I turned into a ridiculous mouse. Even at the prospect of seeing him "socially," I heard myself change on the phone. He heard it, too.

I wanted to see him. I found him attractive. He hadn't flinched when he found out I was an educated woman. He seemed kind and considerate. *I really found him attractive.* And that was the problem. Two problems, in fact. I wanted to be out of the convent and on my own a decent length of time—months—before I began dating men. I wanted a clear separation between leaving the convent and living as an ordinary American woman. And secondly, at thirty, I was as inexperienced as a young girl. He would not expect that. It would make things difficult.

The O'Connors' house was a short drive from the exit on the Southern State Parkway. It was small and boxy, with the lush green lawn and garden that are so common on Long Island. I pulled into their driveway, stopped in front of a one-car garage, and walked to the front door.

It was opened almost immediately.

"Hi," a casually dressed woman with short gray hair said with a smile. "Christine Bennett?"

"That's me." I offered my hand.

"Delores O'Connor. Call me Del."

We shook hands. "I'm Chris."

"Kev's in the living room."

Former detective Kevin O'Connor sat in a reclining chair from which he extricated himself as I approached. We shook hands, made pleasantries, and he asked his wife for a couple of beers. I declined the offer. He got back in his chair, worked the mechanism, and got into position. His wife turned off the TV as she left the room.

"This guy Jack Brooks who called yesterday, he said you were interested in the Talley murder. So how come?"

"I'm doing some research on old murders," I said, having decided this was the best approach. "This one is fascinating because of the twins."

"So where does Brooks fit in?"

"He got the file and found you."

"Uh-huh."

He still had the bright blue eyes, but his body had gone to fat, in spite of his morning golfing. He had a classic beer belly over which was pulled a green golfing shirt that coordinated with his pants. His hair was gray and thinning. Somewhere in the face was the handsome one that Magda had admired forty years ago, but I had to struggle to find it.

"Can I ask you some questions?" I asked.

"Shoot."

"Did the twins ever say anything to you to indicate they were guilty?"

O'Connor's face screwed into a pained expression. "The twins never said nothin'."

"Nothing at all?"

"Didn't gimme the time o' day."

"So you arrested them on the basis of evidence you found in the apartment."

"Yeah. When did that happen again?"

"Nineteen fifty."

"Nineteen fifty, nineteen fifty," he murmured. "Hey, Del?" he called. "When did Mike and me start to be partners?"

"After Carol was born," his wife's voice called from the

kitchen. She appeared in the living room with a can of beer and a glass of iced tea.

"Was that that Easter one?" he asked me.

"The body was discovered on Easter Sunday. The file says the murder probably happened on Good Friday."

"Yeah, right. There was a girl there, like a baby-sitter."

"Magda."

"Yeah, some Polack name. Kinda cute."

"Do you remember what it was that convinced you the twins did it?"

He moved one shoulder in a shrug. "They'd been at 'er. You could see it. There was blood all over. It was a knifing, right?"

"Yes."

"Hell, everything said it was them. They were retards, they got their fingerprints over everything, they were alone with her." His voice ended slightly up, as though there were many other indications of the twins' guilt that he was just too exhausted to enumerate.

"But you were sure they were the ones."

He looked at me quizzically. "You think they weren't?"

"I don't know. I'm just looking into it."

"Oh, hell, sure they did it." He paused to drink some beer and I sipped the iced tea, which was quite tasty. "I had another one, maybe ten years after that, a guy got cut up by a neighbor after a fight over garbage. The neighbor turned out—"

"Kev," his wife interrupted, "I don't think the lady's interested in the other case."

"Oh. Yeah." He started to say something further, but checked himself.

"Did anybody check for blood that wasn't Mrs. Talley's type?"

"I s'pose. That's forensics. The lab guys. Not my job."

"Was there anyone else's blood found there?"

He smiled. "That's a long time ago. Look in the file."

I had, and there hadn't been any other blood at the scene. "If there wasn't any other blood except the victim's, couldn't that mean that someone else did it and cleaned up after himself? That's something the twins wouldn't have done."

"Christ, I don't know what they found there. The guys did it, that's all. Del, you got another beer?"

"Later, Kev."

"Del."

Del got up and left the living room.

"Who was your partner that day, Mr. O'Connor?"

"Call me Kev. You know, I'm tryin' to remember. Geez, that was a long time ago."

I had asked just to test his memory. Magda had recalled every detail of that day; Kevin O'Connor seemed to be coasting on broad recollections. Del returned with a can of beer.

"Was that the Easter I missed dinner at your folks' and your father was so pissed?"

Del grinned. "That was it, hon."

"Geez, he was sore—1950, huh?"

"Did you question the twins yourself?" I asked.

"Sure. It was my case."

"Did you know when you were questioning them that they had very special gifts of memory?"

He looked dazed, as if I'd asked him to solve some difficult mathematical problem. "The girl told me somethin'," he said finally. "I got nothin' outa them. Ab-so-lutely nothin'."

"Did you interview the father?"

"Yeah, I guess." He didn't sound very sure.

"He lived in New Jersey," I prompted.

"Yeah, right."

"Did it occur to you the father might have had a good motive to kill his wife?"

O'Connor looked puzzled again.

"The family cost him money," I said simply.

"Look, honey," O'Connor said, "those twins did it. That's all. A judge said so. The evidence said so. There's no story here."

"Did a psychiatrist ever examine the twins?" I asked.

"We had a guy come over from Kings County. They wouldn't talk."

"Not even to a psychiatrist," I said, more to myself than to him. "Did anyone call in the psychiatrist who had been studying them?"

O'Connor shrugged. "We're in Brooklyn. We'd call Kings County when we needed a shrink."

My iced tea was nearly gone and I was developing a distinct dislike for Kevin O'Connor. I had expected interest and a memory for details. Instead I had encountered a nearly blank wall.

"A man's coat was missing from the coat closet," I said. "What did you think when you were told that?"

"What do ya mean?" Something seemed to change in him—or maybe it was just my hopeful imagination.

"When you heard that an overcoat was missing, did you look for it? Did you think that maybe someone had put it on to cover up a bloody shirt and walked out with it?"

"Hey, wait a minute." Something in his face became alert. "There something in the file on this coat?"

It was a question I couldn't answer, because I hadn't read every document in the file, but the fact that he asked the question made me feel he knew the answer.

"No," I told him. "Magda told me about it."

"The little Polack? C'mon." He smiled in what he must have thought was a winning way.

"She says she told you."

"Hey, I'm a cop, not a nursemaid. A retard goes out and loses his coat, it's not my business. I'm lookin' into a homicide, Chris. Your name Chris?"

I nodded.

"I'm lookin' into a homicide, not a missing coat."

"Magda says she called the station a day or two after Easter Sunday to remind you about it."

"I didn't get no call." He drained his can.

"She says she left a message for you." I was tempted to say, *with a man named Applebaum*, but I couldn't bring myself to.

"She's dreaming." He leaned over toward Del, handing her the empty can. Del took it but didn't move. "I hope you're not suggesting anything, Chris. I was an honest cop, right, Del? I did my job. I put in my time. Sure, I took a cup o' coffee here, a Danish there. But I always had a buck in my hand. They *wanted* me to have it. I never had a complaint made about me. I knew them and they knew me. They were glad when I stopped around to say hello.''

"Kev," Del said, "no one's accusing you."

"No, I want her to know. I want her to know the truth. There wasn't any fuckin' missing coat. That's it. That's the truth. Coupla retards kill their mom, I'm not gonna worry about no fuckin' coat.''

I stood and picked up my bag from the floor. "Thank you," I said. "You've been very helpful."

"Sure." O'Connor was in a snit.

I walked to the door with Del.

"If Kevin says he never heard about a missing coat, he never heard. He's an honest man and he was a good cop," she said.

"Thank you. It was very nice of you to have me over."

I drove into the center of Valley Stream and found a pay phone.

14

I don't own a credit card. Maybe next year, when I've got a brief history of working for a lay institution, I'll apply for one. But in the meantime, I pay for my purchases in cash and I pay for my calls with coins.

I gathered together everything in my change purse and called Jack Brooks. When he got on the phone, I gave him the number I was calling from so he could call me back if I ran out of time.

"Hang up. I'll call you now," he said.

A few seconds later the phone rang.

"I've seen him," I said.

"O'Connor?"

"Yes. I can't say I liked him. He didn't remember half of what Magda remembered. And I think he lied."

"About what?"

"About the missing coat. He changed when I asked about it. He was so convinced the twins were guilty, I don't think he wanted to hear anything that might point in another direction."

"Cops are human," he said. "He wanted to close the case."

"Have you found Applebaum?"

"Not yet."

"When Magda called about the coat, who was she likely to have talked to? Someone at a nearby desk?"

"The call could have been forwarded to the Brooklyn Communications Bureau, the precinct squad, or the borough office."

"I see." I shuddered at the complexity, the number of people involved, the impossibility of finding them at this late date. "Do you know who O'Connor's partner was? He said he couldn't remember."

"It's in the file. I saw the name somewhere. What happens is, the partners take turns. One time O'Connor's catching the cases, the next time his partner catches. Some teams split the tour four hours of catching apiece. It was just chance that O'Connor got it that day."

"Maybe we can find the partner," I said. "Since it wasn't his case, maybe he'd be more open."

"Possibly, but remember, this is a big fraternity. The brothers protect each other."

"Somewhere there's got to be a crack, and I've got to put a wedge in it. Someone took a coat out of that closet and walked out with it."

"Let me see if I can find O'Connor's partner. What are you planning to do next?"

"I want to find out all I can about Patrick Talley. It's too late today, but first thing tomorrow I'm going to New Jersey and walk into churches. I'll bet he got married as soon as his wife died."

"Good luck. Talk to you tomorrow."

The phone rang after I'd finished dinner.

"Hello, Miss Bennett. This is Edwin Hazlett."

The way he said it, I had the feeling I was supposed to recognize his name. "I'm sorry," I said, "do I know you?"

He laughed. "I'm the mayor of Oakwood. I guess I'm not the household word I thought I was."

"Mr. Mayor. Forgive me, it just didn't ring a bell."

"How're you doing on your project?"

"I'm making progress. I'm afraid I can't say much more, but I'm encouraged and I'm continuing."

"Well, that's good news. You will keep me posted, won't you?"

"Of course. You'll be the first to know if I learn anything concrete."

On Wednesday I drove to the George Washington Bridge—it's free leaving New York, but they clip you three dollars coming back—and crossed to New Jersey. Patrick Talley had lived in a town called Leonia, not far from the Jersey side of the bridge. I used a map to find the street, and then I drove down it slowly until I found the house. It was an old brick house with a small second story, two dormer windows above and on either side of the front door. I thought the house was rather pretty. It stood between two other brick houses, both different, both about the same size. In front of the Talley house a brightly colored plastic riding toy stood on the lawn, which was neither as lush nor as well cared for as the O'Connors'.

I made a U-turn and drove back to the corner I had come from. Leonia is a small town directly west of the bridge, past the town of Fort Lee. It's surrounded by a slew of towns: Fort Lee, Englewood, Teaneck, Bogota, Ridgefield Park, and Palisades Park. I had the feeling that people like Patrick Talley and the woman he lived with would want to marry—had probably planned to marry—as soon as they were legally able. I also felt that they wouldn't do it in the church closest to home, because there would be a certain embarrassment attached to their relationship if it became known they had lived together for years without benefit of matrimony.

On the map, Englewood and Teaneck both looked like larger towns than Leonia, but because I was pointed toward Teaneck, I drove in that direction. It proved fortuitous.

The yellow pages gave me the names and addresses of the Roman Catholic churches in the area. The first one couldn't find any record of the Talleys' marriage, searching from Spring 1950 on, so I went to the next one on my list. It was a big old church with a convent on the grounds, and I found myself wondering about the nuns who lived there. After I lit my three candles, I found Father Romero, a smiling, bearded priest who was happy to look into old records—"It gives me a sense of history"—and he quickly found the Talleys' marriage. They had tied the knot in May of 1950, confirming my suspicion that they had married at the first opportunity after the first Mrs. Talley's untimely death.

There was no record of the Talleys as members of any church organizations, which didn't surprise me since they lived in another parish. I thanked the good father and made a contribution to the church building fund, which pleased him.

Then I returned to Leonia. I felt sure that when the Talley children had been born, the parents would have wanted to baptize them, as any parents would. This they could have done in their parish church simply by concealing the fact that they were not married. Then, when they were able to marry, they slipped away to another parish to avoid embarrassment.

There was no record of Patrick Talley Jr. being baptized in the local church, but the daughter, Kathleen, had been, in 1939.

A picture of the Talleys started to emerge. Patrick and Anne had begun living together sometime in the 1930s, perhaps in an apartment. (I would probably never know where, but it didn't matter.) After the birth of their son, they had bought the house in Leonia and become members of the local parish. There was little likelihood that anyone would ask them point-blank if they were married. There are few occasions in life when you're called upon to produce a marriage license. If the Talleys traveled abroad and needed passports, they could probably lie to the feds as well, or tell the truth and use their legal names. It would make little difference. But people didn't travel much during the war, and probably not very much in the years immediately after.

I asked Father McDonald, the priest at the local church, to look further in his records for first communions, organization memberships, and so on. They were all there, until the summer of 1951, little more than a year after the murder, when the Talleys moved to another New Jersey town farther from the bridge and probably, I thought, more fashionable and more expensive.

I was right.

I found the town on the map and drove north along roads with county numbers through a succession of towns, past a reservoir, into communities where the size of the lots was increasingly larger. Suddenly, at a bend in the road, I saw the church ahead of me. It was a frame building one story high with a large parking lot behind it. Inside, I found it divided roughly in half, the church on one side, and a few meeting or classrooms on the other. In one of these rooms a small group of women sat around a table.

"Excuse me," I said, "I'm looking for the pastor."

They looked at each other. "You can probably find him in the rectory," one said.

They directed me and I took off. The rectory was a house on a residential street about a quarter of a mile from the church. The door was opened by a young woman in street clothes who turned out to be Sister Diane. Part of her job was assisting in the parish, and she was more than happy to be helpful.

As it turned out, the Talleys had lived in this small town until Patrick died in 1965. His widow then left for an apartment in White Plains, New York. That piece of information gave me a shiver. Oakwood isn't far from White Plains, and there was a chance Anne Talley might still be alive. She was born in 1907, which would make her about eighty-three. It also made me think that one or both of her children might be living in that area. After all, where do you go when your husband dies? To be near the children.

Sister Diane checked the marriages starting with 1955, when Kathleen Talley would have been seventeen. It was such a small town ("We're over four thousand now," Sister Diane said) that looking at a year's marriage records took less than a minute. And suddenly there it was, Kathleen Talley and Gordon Mackey, June 1958, when the bride was twenty.

"Any forwarding reference?" I asked, so excited I could scarcely contain myself.

"An address in White Plains. Looks like an apartment number. And a letter was sent to the church, introducing them."

"Wonderful." I wrote it all down. "Would you mind looking to see if the son married here? If he married a local girl, it's always possible."

"I don't mind at all. It's kind of fun to see the old names. It's surprising how many are still here after so many years. It's a town people get attached to."

"It's very pretty."

She went right through to the present, but Patrick Jr. hadn't married in town, and there didn't seem to be any reference to him anywhere. But at least I had something to go on.

Before leaving the town, I drove to the Talleys' address to see the house they had lived in. It took my breath away. The contrast between the little brick house with its tiny front lawn and this old colonial set way back from the road, a circular drive in front and stately old trees everywhere, was dramatic. On a lark, I turned in to the drive, parked the car, and went to the front door.

It was opened by a well-dressed woman in her fifties. I introduced myself and told her I was looking for Mrs. Talley, who had lived here in the sixties.

"We bought the house from her," the woman said. "Her husband had died and she was all alone."

"I don't suppose you kept in touch with her."

"We never saw her. I think she left when she put the house up for sale. She wasn't even there at the closing. Her lawyer came. I think it was too painful for her, you know, selling the house she'd raised her children in. We just dealt through the realtors."

"Was the house in good condition when you bought it?"

"Oh yes. No house is perfect, you know, but they'd kept it up. And it was furnished beautifully. It was our first house and it was really a reach for us. We kept her decorations for years, until we could afford to do our own thing."

"Well, thank you. It's really a beautiful house."

"If she's still alive and you find her, tell her we've been good to the house. I think she'd like to hear that."

"I will. Thanks for your help."

I drove around the rest of the half circle of drive, lingered a minute at the tree-shaded road, and went on my way.

Sister Diane had told me how to get to the Tappan Zee Bridge, which crosses the Hudson River farther north than the George Washington. There the toll is only $2.50, so I saved fifty cents on the day. Hah!

The church in White Plains found a record of a baptism for Kathleen and Gordon Mackey's first child, a daughter, Lisa, born in 1961. The family moved after that to an address in North Tarrytown, which was close to the Tappan Zee Bridge, from which I had just come. It was already three o'clock and I had visited more towns in New Jersey than I ever knew existed, not to mention half the Catholic churches on the east coast. When you get up at five, you tend to tire early, and I could feel fatigue gnawing at me. I had done a good day's work and it was time to go home.

I called Information that evening and asked for Gordon Mackey at the address the church in White Plains had given me. He wasn't at that address, but the operator volunteered that someone with that name lived at a different address in the same town. I wrote down the number, hung up, and rallied my courage. I didn't like the idea of calling a stranger—possibly a wrong number, at that—but either I did it, or it didn't get done. I killed a little time by calling Information again and asking for Mrs. Anne Talley or Mrs. Patrick Talley. There was no listing for either name in White Plains.

That left me with a phone number for Gordon Mackey and no excuse not to call. I dialed the number.

A man answered, and I asked for Kathleen Mackey. He asked for my name and I gave it. He said, "Just a minute," and left the phone. I heard his voice at a distance say, "Some gal named Bennett," and then the phone was picked up.

"Hello?"

"Is this Kathleen Mackey?"

"Yes, it is."

"Mrs. Mackey, my name is Christine Bennett and I'm researching some events that happened in 1950."

"What events?" she asked quickly.

"The death of Alberta Talley."

There was a moment of silence. Then, "Who are you? What do you want?"

"I'd just like to get together with you, Mrs. Mackey. I'd like to ask—"

But she cut me off. "Exactly what kind of 'research' are you doing?"

"I'll be glad to tell you about it when I see you. It has to do with the twins." I thought that if I dropped something about the twins, she would know that I was aware of all the family relationships.

"How did you find me?" she blurted.

"In the phone book, actually," I said.

"I have to talk to my brother. Give me your name again."

I did.

"And your phone number."

When she had it, she said she would call me back, and she hung up rather abruptly. I knew I had stirred something up, but I had no idea what. I felt fairly confident that Kathleen Mackey would return my call. She was listed and I could find her. I might not want to impose myself that way, but she didn't know that.

It was nearly nine and I was beat. I turned in.

15

Jack called me Thursday morning, and I gave him an abbreviated version of my day.

"We should send you after Judge Crater. You sure you haven't been doing this all your life?"

"Very sure. But now I'm coming to a standstill. I have to give Kathleen Mackey time to get back to me, and I've talked to pretty much all the people on my list."

"I'm still looking for O'Connor's partner. His name is Stassky. He was about O'Connor's age, so he's probably retired."

"Okay. Then I think I'll come back to Brooklyn this morning and see those two people again, the old man across the street and Selma Franklin. I want to know why they lied."

"Probably has nothing to do with the Talley case."

"But I want to know."

"I'm not discouraging you. Will you have lunch?"

I caught myself smiling. "Sure."

"Whenever you get here. And look, if I'm not here, I do get called away sometimes. I'll give you a rain check."

"Fine."

I arrived at the Talleys' apartment house at nine-thirty. Mrs. Franklin buzzed me in and I took the elevator up to the fourth floor.

"It's nice to see you again," she said, welcoming me. She was wearing a loose-fitting colorful cotton shift that might have been a housedress or might just be the kind of comfortable clothing you wear on a hot day in Brooklyn.

"I'm glad I caught you," I said. "I kind of decided to come on the spur of the moment, and I didn't want to call you too early in the morning to ask if you'd be in."

"You could call at sunrise, I'd be up already." She smiled and plopped into the same chair in the living room she had sat in last time. I took the nearest chair to hers, as I had done on my first visit, making it seem as though this were merely a continuation of that last pleasant conversation.

But for me it was different. I knew now that I was in the identical apartment to the one Mrs. Talley had been murdered in. This was her living room; over there in a kitchen exactly like that one, Mrs. Talley had been murdered.

"You thought of some more questions," Mrs. Franklin stated, inviting me to proceed.

"I found out that the Talleys lived in the apartment above yours," I said.

"That's true." She said it blandly, but I thought I saw her raising her guard.

"Were you home that day?"

"Well, of course, that's what the policeman wanted to know."

I waited.

"It was Good Friday, you know, that day. It's not my holiday, but my children had no school, so it was a holiday for them. What I did that day . . ." She shook her head.

"Some shopping, some sewing. What I told the police is what I did. You want to know if I heard anything."

I nodded.

"Not a thing. Lunch I'm sure we had at home, so I can tell you it didn't happen at lunchtime. Dinner I think we had at my mother's in those days on Friday, so I couldn't tell you about after five-thirty."

"And the rest of the weekend, Saturday and Sunday morning before the police came, did anything sound unusual up there?"

She seemed very wary now, measuring her responses. "Nothing unusual. The same as always."

"What was it like usually?" I asked.

She shrugged, but her face, her round, chubby face, had hardened. "Footsteps," she said. "Nothing special."

"Were you on good terms with Mrs. Talley?"

"I told you. We lived in the same building. We smiled and said 'hello' in the street."

I knew she would never admit anything if I didn't provoke her, but I didn't want to make her angry. She was an old woman and a very unlikely murderer. "They made a lot of noise up there, didn't they?" I said.

She shrugged again. "People make noise when they walk."

"Someone in this apartment used to bang on the ceiling to make them be quiet."

She gave me a hard look, but the corners of her mouth started to curl. "So how come a young girl like you knows something the police don't know?"

"Someone told me."

"Now? Today?"

"A few days ago. The girl that helped Mrs. Talley. She remembered the banging."

"The little blond girl," Mrs. Franklin said.

"Yes."

"Why do you want to know all these things?"

"Because I think someone else killed Mrs. Talley. And to prove it, I need all the information I can get."

She looked straight ahead of her, avoiding my eyes, her mouth set in what I took to mean not determination but resignation. "All right," she said finally, "I'll tell you what I never told anyone else. I didn't get along with her. I lived for twelve years with such noise, it would drive you crazy. Not voices. This is an old building, thick, built solid. Voices you don't hear. But on my head the whole day and half the night, such pounding, you could not believe it. They ran, they jumped, they did I-don't-know-what. A little carpeting would have helped. They didn't have it. My children slept in the room under the twins. Sometimes they couldn't fall asleep. When it got so bad that I couldn't take it anymore, I banged on the ceiling with a broom handle."

"It must have been very unpleasant."

"Terrible."

"You didn't speak to her, did you?"

She shook her head. "In the street we looked the other way."

"You told me a story, Mrs. Franklin, about Mrs. Talley asking the twins what color the light was before they crossed the street." The same story had appeared, almost verbatim, in the police interview. "Did you make it up?"

"I didn't make it up. It's a true story. Remember I told you my best friend, Harriet Cohen, lived next door to them? Next door is not underneath. Next door was quiet. She was friendly with Mrs. Talley, my friend Harriet. The story I told you, I heard from her."

"I see."

"Christine. May I call you Christine?" I nodded. "I didn't hate the woman. I hated the noise. I didn't want her dead. When I heard on Sunday what happened, I cried. Do you believe it? You say things sometimes you don't mean and then something terrible happens and you feel—" she paused "—responsible."

"It wasn't your fault."

"Your head knows this, but it hurts all the same."

"So you heard nothing unusual that day," I said.

"Unusual. Who knows what unusual is when every day it

sounds like a stampede? How many times did I say, 'Someone must be getting killed up there'? So when it happened on that bad Friday, everything was the same as always.''

"Thank you for being so honest, Mrs. Franklin."

"I didn't even give you tea."

"You gave me something much better."

"You're such a nice girl. Come in and say hello if you're in the neighborhood."

I rang a second time at Mrs. Cappicola's house before I heard her footsteps approaching. She opened the door, recognized me, and said, "My father isn't home."

"It's you I'd like to talk to, Mrs. Cappicola."

She looked for a moment as though she were considering this. Then she said, "Come in, Sister."

We went into the same living room and sat.

"I really don't think I can tell you any more. We weren't involved in what happened across the street."

"I know that. But I was looking over my notes the other night and I noticed your father referred to the 'blue-and-white' police cars. They weren't blue and white in 1950. They were green and white."

"Well, you know, he's an old man and his memory isn't what it used to be."

There was a definite creak overhead, as though someone had moved on the second floor. I glanced up toward the ceiling, and Mrs. Cappicola looked pained. This seemed to be my morning for making people unhappy.

"Did he really see those police cars?" I asked. "Was he really here that day?"

"He was here." But that was all she said, as though that had answered both my questions.

"And he saw what happened across the street?"

She sat in the chair looking nowhere. Finally she said, "He didn't look out of the window all day."

"I see."

"You don't see. When you came last week, I forgot that was the year . . . My father is a devout Catholic, Sister. Even today, at his age, he goes to mass every Sunday. That Easter, in 1950, he missed mass for the only time in his adult life.''

''I didn't mean to stir up old problems. You don't have to explain.'' I started to put my notebook away. What difference did it make whether one old man had looked out his window that Easter Sunday?

''He had a terrible fight with my brother,'' she went on, as though I had not spoken. Upstairs, there were rhythmic creaks, and I thought her father was probably rocking in a chair. ''My brother is much older, and he'd gotten in trouble that weekend. It was nothing serious, but my father reacted very strongly. There was such shouting that weekend, and then, on Easter Sunday morning, I thought my father would kill him. My mother grabbed me and took me to church while they were still fighting. They never went. Neither one of them.''

''I'm sorry I upset you, Mrs. Cappicola.''

''He never went near the window the whole day. He was afraid someone he knew might see him and wonder why he hadn't been to church.'' She smiled. ''We worry about silly things, don't we?''

''I'm afraid we do.''

''I went out on the sidewalk to watch what was going on. People gathered. There were rumors about what had happened. When the pictures were in the paper the next day, it was like I was part of something very important.''

''You were.'' I got up, sorry I had come. ''I hope your father and your brother came to terms.''

''Oh yes, later they did. He's a good man, my brother. A good son. But it was the only mass my father ever missed.''

I thanked her and left. Crossing the street, I felt sure the old man on the second floor was watching me.

16

We went to the same place for lunch and were waited on by the same waitress. There was something different about Jack Brooks this time, the way he looked at me. He kept smiling when our eyes met, and it made me smile back.

I told him about Selma Franklin's new story.

"You've got to expect that, that people'll lie to protect themselves. Whoever questioned her after that murder should've been more sensitive to the situation. Anyone who lives in an apartment in New York knows that the lady downstairs can't stand the noise from upstairs. It's the way things are."

"So the place to live is on the top floor."

"Then the roof leaks," he said, and I laughed.

"Always?"

"Always in New York."

"You don't think that sweet little lady could have reached the end of her rope and gone upstairs and killed Mrs. Talley?"

"I doubt it. What would you do if you convinced yourself she did?"

"I don't know," I said truthfully. It would be much easier to show that someone dead and buried had been guilty or to find that a dirty old man who had done other terrible things had done this one, too. "I wonder if you can check something for me." I pulled out my notes to get the spelling right. "Sometime that weekend the son of the old man across the street got into some kind of trouble. His sister told me about it this morning. She didn't say what kind of trouble, but I

101

had the feeling it was more serious than she wanted to let
on.''

Jack pulled a folded piece of paper from his pocket, found
a clean surface, and clicked his pen open. ''Got a name?''

''Antonetti.''

''I'll try to have it when I see you Saturday.'' He turned
the folded paper until he found what he was looking for.
''Applebaum,'' he said. ''Applebaum Sr. never worked in
Brooklyn, so I guess he's not the guy your Magda talked to.''

''We'll have to look for a different fruit.''

''You know, looking for fruits in the police department is
not the way I want to be remembered.''

I started to say something that I hoped would sound clever,
but he interrupted. ''I like your hair. It has a devil-may-care
look about it.''

''It was cut by a friend. I need a more professional hand.''

He ran a hand through his own rather wildly curly mass
of hair. ''Don't we all. So you found Patrick Talley's daughter.''

''I spoke to her,'' I told him, ''just last night.'' I told him
of my trip to New Jersey and all my inquiries.

''Not bad,'' he said appreciatively when I had finished.
''You think he's the man, don't you?''

''Except that the twins didn't identify him, which I really
can't explain. But if you had seen the contrast between the
little house they first lived in and the place they moved up
to, you'd know why I feel that way. And everything fell into
place. His wife dies and he marries his lover. A year later
the family moves to a minimansion and they furnish it ex-
pensively. He was maintaining two families for years, and
one day in 1950 he suddenly had only one. No one else
benefited the way he did.''

''But he's dead and buried.''

I nodded. ''And I have qualms about naming a dead man
who can't defend himself.''

''Well, we'll see what you turn up when you talk to the
daughter.''

We walked back to the precinct together and made arrangements for Saturday night. Then I drove back to Oakwood.

Kathleen Mackey called at six just as I was about to sit down to a quick dinner. I turned off the stove as I passed it on my way to the telephone.

"Miss Bennett, this is Kathleen Mackey," she announced.

"Thank you for calling," I said, trying to sound friendly.

"You know, summer is really a very bad time to get together. My brother is leaving for vacation tomorrow—the Fourth is next week, you know—and I'm involved in a number of activities that don't leave me much free time."

Her tone was patronizing, and her excuses sounded like quick fixes. But I couldn't lose her now and I couldn't let her postpone this meeting till after the summer. After the summer I was finished, so far as Greenwillow was concerned.

"I could see you tonight," I said, taking a bold step.

"Well, that seems rather—hold on a minute." She covered the mouthpiece and I could hear muffled noises. "I'll call you back," she said suddenly, and hung up.

I went back to the stove and tried to repair my dinner. I had everything out on the table when the phone rang again.

"When could you be here?" Kathleen Mackey asked without preliminaries.

"In half an hour." I looked at the dinner that I would not be able to eat.

"No. That's too soon. How's—" She covered the phone again. "Could you make it at eight?"

"Yes."

"I can't give you much time."

"I'll make it as fast as I can."

She gave me the address and some brief directions and hung up. I waltzed back to the kitchen table, almost too excited to eat. I had done it.

I got there early, found the house, and drove away so that I could arrive at the stroke of eight. When I returned, a car had parked in the previously empty driveway. I left mine on the street and walked to the front door.

The house was in a beautiful community near the Hudson River. It was a long way from the little house in Leonia and a longer way from Alberta Talley's apartment in Brooklyn.

Kathleen Mackey was a good-looking woman. I knew from the police records that she was fifty-two, and her brother two years older. She was slim and well dressed in a khaki outfit with rolled-up sleeves, a wide belt of some endangered reptile's expensive skin, and attractive sandals. She led me into a room with sliding glass doors open onto a large deck, where a man sat on a chair that matched a whole set of outdoor furniture.

"Nice to meet you," Patrick Talley Jr. said genially, raising himself without offering his hand and returning quickly to his seat.

"Thank you. I'm Christine Bennett."

"Kath tells me you're doing some research or something on an old murder."

"The murder of Alberta Talley in 1950." I sat down at the umbrellaed table, took my notebook and pen out of my bag, and flipped to a clean page. I noticed Kathleen's face as I did so. Her eyes seemed to open wide and burn through my notebook.

"We probably can't help you," Patrick said. "Never knew the lady." He at least had a cordial sound to his voice.

I wondered how much he resembled his father. I imagined his father as something of a charmer, perhaps because I have a stereotype of the successful salesman in my head.

"Do you know when your parents started living together?" I asked, looking directly at him.

"Before I was born, that's for sure. I guess in the mid-thirties. They didn't talk about it much. Lots of people lived together in those days. Common-law kind of thing."

"Did he visit his first family?"

"He did not," Kathleen's icy voice shot at me. We were all sitting equidistant from one another around the circular table so that everyone was almost opposite everyone else.

"Do you know if he ever telephoned, if he kept any relationship going with them?"

"Got me," Patrick said. He smiled, and I felt sure he had decided to be nice to me but give me nothing of value. It was clear that tonight he was the family spokesman. "I didn't hang around when Dad was on the phone."

"What kind of research are you doing that requires questions like these?" Kathleen asked.

"I'm looking into some unsolved murders."

"But that one was solved," she shot back.

"There was no trial, no conviction. It's possible the twins didn't kill their mother."

"And you think my father did!" Her voice rose in shock and anger.

"I don't know who did. I'm trying to get as complete a picture as I can of the family. It's part of my research." I hoped it sounded legitimate. "Do you remember how old your father was when he retired?" I looked back at Patrick.

"Well, you know, Dad sold insurance and he was good at it. He wasn't the kind to stay home just because he reached a certain age. He kept some clients till he was well into his seventies."

"That must have been nice for him," I said.

It was growing dark. Someone inside the house must have flicked a switch at that moment, because lights went on, not just on the deck, but along the perimeter of the property. It would be a lovely place to have a summer evening party.

"It was nice for everybody," Patrick said. "He kept up his business, but they had time to travel and do a lot of things they wanted."

"He must have lived to a ripe old age with a regimen like that."

"He surely did," Patrick said. "They took him kicking and screaming."

I smiled. "Where is your father buried?" I asked.

"How dare you ask a question like that," Kathleen said.

"Come on, Kath," her brother cajoled. "Actually, they

were on vacation when Dad died, and Mom had him buried
there.''

That surprised me. ''What an unusual thing to do,'' I said.

''Well, they had a little bungalow they used to go to. R
and R. You know.''

I suddenly started picking up interesting vibes. Neither of
them had said where Patrick Sr. was buried, and something
was very strange. I couldn't imagine the Talleys living in a
''little bungalow,'' and I found it very peculiar that, wher-
ever he had died, he had not been buried somewhere near
home with a funeral at the local church near their New Jersey
home. ''What country is that?'' I asked.

Patrick smiled. He didn't want to answer, but he couldn't
avoid the question. ''The Bahamas, I think it was,'' he said
finally. ''Isn't that so, Kath?''

She said, ''Yes,'' tightly, and I sensed she was seething.

''Grand Bahama Island, that's it,'' he said.

''What a nice place to have a bungalow,'' I said, hoping I
didn't sound sarcastic. ''Does your mother spend all her time
there now or might I be able to find her here?''

''Stay away from my mother,'' Kathleen ordered, letting
me know that Anne was still alive. ''She had nothing to do
with my father's first wife. There's nothing she can tell you.''

''It must have come as a terrible shock to your father when
he heard his wife was dead.''

''In a lot of ways,'' Patrick said, recovering his calm demeanor. ''With cops knocking on the door, my parents had
to tell us a lot of things they would have rather not. It wasn't
an easy time for them.''

''And of course, you've never had anything to do with the
twins.''

''Nothing at all. Don't even know if they're still alive.''

''They are,'' I said. ''I've visited one of them recently.''

''No kidding,'' Patrick said in a flat tone.

''How did your lives change after the murder?'' I asked.

''Nothing changed,'' Kathleen said firmly.

''Well, that's not true,'' her brother said in that easy manner he had. ''As I said, we found out things we hadn't known

before, that we had these—half-brothers, that Dad had had a wife, and eventually that the folks weren't married. It was a shocker, I'll tell you.''

"Did he ever talk about them?''

"Not too much. As you can imagine, it hadn't been the happiest of marriages.''

"Because of the twins?''

"Because of the twins and because of their mother,'' Kathleen said in her icy tone. "How would you like to come home every night to a family like that? My father pleaded with her to put those boys away, to let them have a real life together without those terrible encumbrances. They couldn't go to a goddamn movie without getting a baby-sitter. Their lives revolved around those boys. There was nothing else and she wouldn't have it any other way.'' I could hear Kathleen's anger mounting as she warmed to her tale. "My father was a kind, warm person. He was loving, he had a sense of humor. She took all that away from him. She made him into a robot whose only reason for living was to support that family. And what did he get from them? Nothing.'' She spat out the word. "He had to leave her to save himself.''

"C'mon, Kath,'' her brother coaxed.

"No, let me say it. The only thing in the world that woman cared about was those two retarded sons of hers, and if you ask me, she got what was coming to her. She was a leech. When I found out how much my father was sending her every month, I realized why we had to live the way we did. She had money for everything, and we had to count pennies.''

"It must have gotten much better after she died,'' I said, hoping for a reaction before she thought better of it.

"Of course it did. And when my father got his—''

"Kathleen!'' It was the first time Patrick had spoken sharply. "I'm sure Miss Bennett doesn't want to hear personal details.''

I did, of course, but there was no way of making her continue. She sat back in her chair, seemingly stunned by what she had nearly said.

To my surprise, she smiled. "Is your research complete now?"

"I think I have a better picture of things," I said. I closed my book and pushed my chair back. "Thank you both very much. You've been very helpful." That was my understatement of the year.

17

I slept on it, reserving thought until the next morning, Friday, when I went out for my daily lope. But I had scarcely reached the corner when Melanie Gross came out of her house and joined me.

"Hi, good morning," she called, coming down her driveway in running clothes.

"Good morning."

"I tried to call you yesterday. You're *never* home, do you know that?"

"It occurs to me when I run out of milk and eggs."

"I wanted to ask you . . . I really don't know how to say this, but would you like to go out with a cousin of mine?"

"You mean on a date?"

"Sure. He's a terrific person, works on Wall Street, has lots of money, a great apartment in New York. *I'd* go out with him if I were single. He's Jewish, of course. I don't know how you feel about that."

I laughed. "People are people. Do you think I could take a rain check? I've only been out of the convent a month now, and I told myself I should wait a few months before I start to think of men as men. I mean, I'd kind of like to get my sea legs before I plunge in.'' The longer I babbled, the more I was apt to mix my tenuous metaphors.

"Okay," Melanie said. "I'll ask you again in the fall. He'll probably still be around. He works so hard, he never has time to do much else. My aunt is having fits over it.''

I said something noncommittal and changed the subject to my advancing investigation.

When I got home, I made breakfast and took it out to the dining room so that I could get an early start on my thinking. The Bahamas had rung a bell as soon as Patrick Talley Jr. had mentioned it last night. People with money to hide went to the Bahamas. Perhaps Patrick Sr. had cheated the IRS and wanted a place to stash his funds. I hadn't for a minute believed the "bungalow" story. As I thought about it, I had an idea.

I took my coffee cup back into the kitchen, called Information for the area code for Grand Bahama Island, and reached Information there in a few seconds.

"I'd like the number for Patrick Talley," I told the operator who had answered with a pleasing lilt.

She came back quickly. "There's no number for Mr. Patrick.''

"What about Mrs. Patrick or Anne?"

"One moment.''

I waited, hoping.

"Yes, Mrs. P. is here." She gave me the street and number, and I thanked her and hung up.

I looked at the address she had given me for a minute, then looked up the Grosses' number and dialed. Mel answered right away.

"Mel, it's Chris Bennett. I know this is a crazy time to call, but do you know the Bahamas at all?"

"We went to Bermuda once, but that's about it.''

"Did anyone you know ever go there or would you know someone who's familiar with the island?"

"Let's see, my uncle and aunt vacation there sometimes. Should I call him?"

"Would you?''

"Sure. What do you want to know?"

I gave her the Talley address and said I wanted to know what the neighborhood was like.

"I'll get him at the office today."

"Wonderful. And, Mel, if he needs to call someone in the Bahamas, I'll pay for the call. It's really important."

"On my uncle's phone bill, a call to the moon wouldn't be noticed. But I'll relay your offer."

I thanked her and went back to my papers.

I spent a couple of hours looking at what I had and didn't have. I didn't have a report on the Antonetti boy, but that might amount to nothing. I didn't have Kevin O'Connor's partner yet. I didn't have the man with the fruitlike name who had taken Magda's message to O'Connor that a man's overcoat was missing from the Talley closet. But all of these things seemed fairly inconsequential.

What I had was interesting but ultimately led me nowhere. I had Selma Franklin, who had lived underneath the Talleys in 1950 and didn't get along with Mrs. Talley because of the noise the Talleys made. I had Mr. Antonetti, who had lied about seeing what went on so that he wouldn't have to admit he had missed Easter Sunday mass. Scratch that, I thought. Nothing there. I had Magda's story, backed up by a photo in a newspaper, that a coat had been missing from the closet when the twins were arrested. That was something. Add to that Detective O'Connor's abrupt change of demeanor when I brought up the missing coat, and I was sure it was important. I had a psychiatrist's educated opinion that James Talley had not killed his mother.

And I had Patrick Talley, the one person in the world who really benefited from the death of his wife and incarceration of his sons. There was no question in my mind that his then companion, Anne Garfield, would have lied to the police about what time he came home on Good Friday to protect him—whether she knew he had done it or not. If he had driven into New York after his business lunch, he could easily have killed his wife and made it back home in time for dinner (a thought I found repelling). It was probably no more than an hour's drive from the George Washington Bridge to Ocean Avenue near King's Highway in Brooklyn. And with Alberta out of the way, he was free to marry Anne—which he did— was able to buy a better house—which he did—was in a position to live a more sumptuous life—which he obviously had.

Then there was the Bahamas connection. Was I just becoming unduly suspicious or was there something very peculiar about Patrick Talley's death? As a matter of fact, I didn't really know when he had died. *I knew when Anne Talley sold the house.* Patrick might have died long before— or he might still have been alive in the vacation "bungalow" on Grand Bahama Island.

But where did this leave me? I had gotten all I could from the Talley children. Perhaps I could get someone in the Bahamas to look up the date of Patrick's death, but so what?

I sat back and looked at the array of paper on the table. I was now certain the twins had not killed their mother, and I had one good suspect who was dead over twenty years and buried in a foreign country. And I had talked to almost everyone who had had anything to do with the case. Jack Brooks had been helpful, but he doubted that I would turn up anything conclusive. I needed another point of view, a person who looked at the world differently, uniquely.

I went to the kitchen, sat on a chair, and dialed a number from memory.

A familiar voice answered. "St. Stephen's Convent, Sister Angela speaking."

"Angela," I said happily. "I'm so glad to hear your voice. This is—" And then I faltered. "This is Christine Bennett," I said finally, and added, "Sister Edward Frances."

"He*llo*," Angela's sweet voice came back. "How *are* you?"

"Fine, happy, getting used to things."

"Oh, I'm so glad I'm on bells today or I might have missed you. What can I do for you?"

"I'd like to talk to Mother Joseph—if she isn't busy."

"Hold on. I saw her go to her office a little while ago. Let me see if she'll take your call."

There was a click and I waited. Angela had just graduated from St. Stephen's College, was one of the more recent additions to the convent and a very promising one. I had smiled when she said she was "on bells." I hadn't heard that expression for answering the phone and door since I'd left.

I had asked to speak to the General Superior—that's the new designation, by the way—for a special reason. When you enter St. Stephen's, you are assigned a spiritual director, a nun who is older, hopefully wiser, someone who can lead you, listen to you, guide you. It was my good fortune to have Sister Joseph, then a young woman in her thirties, as mine. Today, fifteen years later, she was serving her first term as General Superior of the convent, an indication of the esteem of the nuns who had elected her.

"She'll talk to you," Angela said, returning to the line.

"Thanks, honey."

And then Joseph's calm, assured voice said, "Christine, I wondered how long it would be before I heard your voice again."

We had a brief chat and then I told her I had a problem to discuss with her. She was planning to visit her family for the Fourth of July weekend, which started Wednesday, an awkward day, and eventually we agreed on Sunday. I would drive up for dinner at noon and stay to thrash out my problem. When I hung up, I had the feeling I was on the way to an answer.

At eleven I called Melanie again. "Hal is a lawyer, isn't he?" I asked.

"Right. He's with a firm in Manhattan."

"I'd like to know how to get some information on a will that was probated a long time ago."

"Come on over about eight tonight. We'll have coffee and something and you can talk."

"I'll bring the something."

"Aren't you a dear," Melanie said.

I was just getting ready to find Aunt Meg's old lawn mower (before the town of Oakwood cited me for being unkempt) when the phone rang. It was Jack.

"Got something for you," he said. "I located O'Connor's partner."

"You did?"

"I talked to him a few minutes ago. Name's Herb Stassky and he lives in Florida. Got a pencil?"

"In my hand."

He gave me the number. "How's six-thirty tomorrow?"

"Fine. Call if you get lost."

"I won't," he said ambiguously. "See you tomorrow."

I pressed the switch hook and waited, then lifted my finger and got a dial tone. If Herb Stassky had been at home when Jack called, I might as well see if he was still in. I dialed the number.

A man answered on the second ring.

"Is this Herb Stassky?"

"Yup."

I introduced myself.

"You the gal looking into that old murder?"

"I'm the one. If you have a moment, I'd like to ask you a couple of questions."

"Sure."

I gave him a little background to refresh his memory, which seemed to be somewhat stronger than O'Connor's had been. Then I said, "When you were ready to take the twins down to the station, one of their overcoats was missing. Do you remember that?"

"Yeah, kinda."

"The girl who was there, the baby-sitter, she's the one who noticed it."

"The little blonde with the accent?"

"That's the one."

"Yeah, she said somethin'."

"Did you make a note of that, that there was a coat missing?"

"Y'know, you should talk to Kevin about that. It was his case."

"But you were his partner."

I heard him let out his breath, rippling his lips. "What difference does it make? The case was open-and-shut."

"Are you sure of that?"

"Kevin was."

"So you didn't bother to write down that a man's coat was missing." I stated it.

"Look, you want the truth? It wasn't my case and I figure those twins did it. They're probably dead and buried by now, but—"

"They're not. They're alive. They're sixty-nine years old."

"Jeez." He paused, then said, "Jeez," again. "Well, whatever, I thought it should go in the file that the coat was missing. The girl was so sure. But O'Connor said it would just hold things up. That's it. I left it out. I thought about it, you know? But it wasn't my case and there wasn't anyone else could've killed her."

"So O'Connor told you not to include it."

"It was his case."

I figured that was the closest I would get him to say it. "The girl, Magda, she told me she left a message for O'Connor a day or two later about the coat."

"Yeah, I saw it. Guy named Petrie took it."

"Who?" I asked.

"Petrie." He pronounced it Pea-Tree, *Peachtree*! "He was a friend of mine, that's how come I remember. Petrie and me, we used to have a beer together after work sometimes. He got shot in the sixties and went out on three-quarters disability pension."

"Mr. Stassky, were you as convinced as Detective O'Connor that the twins were guilty?"

"Sure I was," he said without hesitating.

"Even after Magda pointed out that the coat was missing?"

"Look, nothing is ever perfect unless you see it happen yourself. Every case has inconsistencies. Ask anybody, they'll tell you. Nothing fits a hundred percent. You do the best with what you have. So a coat was missing. Maybe one o' those guys went out and left it somewhere. They were mentals, for God's sake. We asked them—you know how long we asked them? The girl told us they were like retarded geniuses; they could remember everything that ever happened in their whole life. So why didn't they tell us if someone else did it? Because they did it and they were hiding the truth. You're right, we shoulda put the missing coat in the file. But we didn't and it happened a hundred years ago.''

I thanked him and got off the phone. I was sorry I had upset him, but the call had been worth it. He had confirmed Magda's story down to the barest detail.

I spent the rest of Friday mowing the lawn and shopping for household necessities. In the evening, armed with a cherry pie from a local bakery, I went to the Grosses'.

I learned a lot from Hal that night about court-appointed lawyers and probating wills. It had occurred to me while I was talking to the Talleys that Mrs. Talley might have had a will, and even if she didn't, she had a diamond ring and a fur coat and maybe a small bank account. I wanted to find out who had inherited it. Hal said I shouldn't bother going to Brooklyn to make the search. He had a cousin who was home from law school for the summer who would probably love the chance to do it herself. He made the phone call while I was there, and she agreed. She would go down first thing Monday morning.

The next day was Saturday, the day of my first date. I opened my closet door first thing in the morning, saw the yellow dress, and knew it was wrong. Nervous as a kid, I did something I had never imagined doing in my life: I spent the whole day buying a dress and a pair of shoes after having my hair cut.

18

Jack arrived punctually at six-thirty. I had the feeling he had done what I had two nights earlier when I went to see Kathleen Mackey, find the place, leave, and return at the appointed time.

"You live in a whole house," he said as he entered the small foyer.

"My aunt died a few months ago and left it to me." I walked into the living room, conscious of my clothes, of myself as a single woman going to dinner with a man. The dress was a fluid silk, beige or tan or some such color and white, with a longish skirt.

A friend who had left the convent several years earlier had offered practical suggestions when I told her of my imminent departure. You could always spot ex-nuns, she said, because they have no sense of color, no idea what matches what. She told me to stick to solid colors and *stay away from polyester*. "That's all they wear," she said, "stuff that goes into the wash and back on the body." I had scrupulously bought only natural fibers since starting my new life.

"Where did you live before?" He sat on the sofa as I sat on a nearby chair. He was wearing a summer suit with a white shirt and a dark silk tie with a small pattern, a drastic change from his casual work clothes.

"Up the Hudson, near where I was teaching."

"Better down here," he said. "Easier winters."

"May I offer you a drink?" Aunt Meg had left a cabinetful of almost antique bottles of liquor, most of them opened but rarely used.

"We'll have something when we get where we're going. You ready?"

"Yes."

"Let's go. I've got some interesting things to tell you."

So at age thirty, I, Christine Marie Bennett, had my first date. I thought later that I couldn't have chosen a better person to have it with, and nervous as I was, I didn't disgrace myself. Probably that was because I knew him a little, liked him a little, and had plenty to talk to him about.

We drove to a restaurant overlooking the Long Island Sound. I'm not sure whether we were in New York or Connecticut, but it didn't matter. It was beautiful, the weather was perfect, and I was so excited about where I was and what I was doing that the next morning I couldn't remember what I'd had to eat.

I do remember that after we had ordered drinks, Jack pulled out one of his famous folded pieces of paper. He opened it once, bent it back so that it stayed open, and said, "I've got something about Paul Antonetti."

"He did get in trouble with the police."

"Sure did. He mugged a little old lady and snatched her purse."

"When?"

"About four in the afternoon on April seventh."

"April seventh was Good Friday."

"Which probably added to his old man's ire."

"Did he use a weapon?" I asked, almost holding my breath.

Jack smiled as though he'd been waiting for the question. "How's a switchblade?"

"A knife," I said, feeling that rush of excitement that a good discovery can bring on. "Was she cut?"

"Only scared. She gave him her purse and he ran. There's a note that the purse was recovered a few days later. He'd tossed it in some garbage after taking the money."

"I guess she didn't say that his shirt was covered with blood."

"Not in the file. She would have if she'd seen it."

"But the time doesn't fit," I said, thinking it through. "If he was arrested at four, either he'd already killed Mrs. Talley and he'd be covered with her blood, or he couldn't have done it later because he was in the police station."

"He wasn't picked up till Saturday."

I stared at him. "Then how . . . ?"

"The woman reported the theft right after it happened. By accident, she saw him in the street the next day, flagged an RMP patrol car, and they took him in. Plenty of time for him to have changed his clothes. If you really think a kid did it."

"He's the only person so far who would have known the twins were retarded but very likely wouldn't have known they were savants."

"So you think he went on a Good Friday rampage."

"It's certainly possible."

"Remember, nothing was taken from the Talley apartment—except the coat. If burglary was his motive, he changed his mind."

"He got scared," I said. "He hadn't expected blood, not to mention murder. When he saw what he'd done, he ran."

"By the way—" he looked down at his paper again "—his alleged knife was never found."

"Then how . . . ?"

"The woman's testimony. She heard the click as he opened it. She saw it. He denied ever having a knife. And by the way, his father made his bail. Cash. He must've kept a lot in the house."

We had been sipping our drinks as we talked. Now the waiter handed us menus. I laid mine down without looking at it. "Poor Mr. Antonetti," I said. "That must have been the worst weekend of his life."

Through the beginning of the meal I told Jack about my conversation with the Talley brother and sister. He made a few comments and then said he would try to find Paul Antonetti, indicating to me that he thought the boy was a possible suspect. Then, quite suddenly, we stopped talking about the case and started talking about ourselves. I felt very comfortable with him. We seemed to share a lot of the values that people need to share if they are to trust each other, if they are to be friends.

As we talked, I felt that I was the one holding back the most. I didn't lie to him, I just neglected to tell him that I'd spent the last fifteen years in a convent. I think I did that because I wanted him to think of me as he would any other American woman—single, college-educated, a teacher—without the stereotypes that being a nun might suggest. I certainly didn't want him to know that this was my first date with a man. Looking back as I drove to St. Stephen's the next day, I felt quite sure that I had carried it off.

We kept talking after the food was gone and the coffee had been poured several times. Finally we left the restaurant and walked along a stretch of the Sound. It was a warm, clear night. Jack took my arm. He told me he was starting law school in the fall, again by taking night classes. It would take years—four anyway—but he didn't care. It was another step forward, and he was a man who didn't stay in one place very long.

He moved his hand up and down my arm, a nice feeling, a man touching me because I was a woman. I knew that men and women slept together on first encounters, that they slept together once and went their separate ways, and I wondered how women could bear such burdens. I liked this man, and I could not imagine joining my body with his and never seeing him again.

What I felt was an eagerness to be near him, a sense that this was something good that I had missed in my life. I am not a person with regrets for things done or not done. I feel sadness at some things that have happened—I wish my mother had lived longer—but I have never felt that a decision made thoughtfully should be discarded loosely and later disparaged. I spent fifteen good and useful years at St. Stephens, but tonight I was happy to be where I was, doing what I was doing.

When we got back to my house, he walked me to the door

and said nice things to me. It wasn't hard to say them back
to him. When the door was unlocked and pushed open, he
stepped inside and kissed me. I suppose if you're fourteen
or sixteen when that happens, you may one day forget the
sensation and the feelings evoked. I know I never will.
Whichever way my life takes me from here, I will remember
that moment, that kiss, that very wonderful man.

I slept till eight and woke up happy.

19

St. Stephen's is one of the most beautiful places on earth.
I say that unequivocally, having seen almost nothing else of
the world. But those heavy, somber old buildings, the vast
green meadows, the trees of immense girth that, as strip-
lings, saw settlers sail up the Hudson, make that enclave
more beautiful than anything I have seen to date.

I arrived well before the dinner hour to give me time to
visit the villa. The villa is home to old and infirm nuns who
need care but not hospitalization. At least one of the residents
was already there when I entered St. Stephen's, but I had a
special friend I particularly wanted to see today.

I parked the car and walked along the flagstone path, by-
passing the front door and rounding the corner of the building. Sister Benedict was sitting in a shaded spot near the
back entrance. She saw me coming and fixed her eyes on
me. Before I left the convent, she had celebrated her eightieth
birthday. She lives in the villa because arthritis has twisted
her hands and made her body painful.

"I knew you'd come back," she called as I approached.
"Where are you staying?"

"I'm just visiting Sister Joseph today, to talk about something."

"If you can't live without us, why don't you try to live with us again?"

I pulled a chair over and sat beside her. "You're looking quite merry," I said, ignoring her question.

"And feeling so. What about you? How's that little house of yours in Oakville or Briarwood or whatever they name those towns?"

"Oakwood. It's a wonderful house. I mowed the lawn this week for the first time."

"They'll run you out of town if you don't keep it nice."

"That's why I mowed." I looked around. "Is everyone away on vacation? It seems so empty."

"They're here and there. Fourth of July is this week. How are you keeping yourself?"

"I'm getting ready to teach a course this fall on Poetry and the Contemporary American Woman."

"What do you know about her?"

"I am one," I said, thinking that last night had been an entering point.

"You look like one," Sister Benedict said. She smiled and pulled my hand onto her lap with her own two gnarled ones. "You look happy."

"I am."

"Then you did the right thing."

"Thank you."

We chatted for a while and then I excused myself and walked to the chapel. Two novices crossed my path, walking with their eyes down and their hands crossed in their sleeves. Seeing them brought back old memories.

The chapel was empty and cool. I lit three candles, then walked down to the altar, looking at the interior as a visitor might. I recognized the altar cloths as the work of Sister Grace, the most talented embroiderer in the order. I remember when, as a novice, it had been my charge to wash, starch, and iron those beautiful cloths, and then roll them up in cylinders to avoid folds. It was a task that I had enjoyed, one of those mindless things we do that leave our brains free to think of other things.

From the chapel I went to the community room in the Mother House. Several nuns were sitting around, waiting for dinner. I heard someone say, "Kix!" and I went to say a warm hello. At five to twelve we started for the dining room, I the only one in street dress. I was surrounded by the brown Franciscan habit.

The nuns went first to their respective drawers and took out their napkin rings. It was Sunday and they would have fresh napkins today, which they would replace in their drawers after dinner. Those drawers were also where we found our mail each afternoon, where messages were left for us. I wondered who would inherit my drawer.

Mother Joseph met me in the dining room, and we sat down and ate an excellent Italian meal cooked by a nun from an Italian family. I had never learned much about cooking and always enjoyed these special meals.

When dinner was over, I spent a few minutes greeting the nuns I had not seen earlier, and then Joseph and I went up to her office.

Her office was on the second floor, where the ceiling sloped down to meet the outside wall. She had a desk that was as messy as her mind was clear. A long conference-style table served as an overflow for her papers. As she tidied a place for us, I went to the window facing west and looked out between two huge trees, straining to see the mythical view of the Hudson, but it was not there.

"Come and sit down," Joseph said, "and let's hear what you have to say."

It took the better part of an hour for me to explain the facts of the murder and to detail everything I had learned in ten days of asking questions. Joseph listened, asking few questions, writing down names here and there on a blank sheet of unlined paper in an order that made no apparent sense to me. When I was finished, she looked up. Her face, framed in the veil, had the same calm look of self-assurance that I had admired when I first met her. She looked reflective for a moment, and then she slowly began shaking her head.

"There may be an answer in these people you've been talking to," she said finally, "but there may not. What interests me most is the twins. Where did their gifts go between Good Friday morning and Easter Sunday?"

"They were traumatized," I said, hearing myself use the word yet another time and feeling oddly embarrassed by it. "They were separated."

"The psychiatrist said—"

Joseph raised her hand. "Wait. These tricks they performed, did they do them separately or together?"

"I don't really know. I was told they were being studied because it was so unusual to find twin savants."

"And since that incident, they've never been together, have they?"

"I don't think so."

"The police wouldn't have let them stay together. They might have made up a story to protect themselves. At least, that's how the police would see it."

"Probably."

"And nothing has shaken their silence in forty years." She closed her eyes a moment. "You said they had deteriorated."

"Besides losing their special gifts, they no longer speak very much, they can't tie their shoelaces anymore, they even have difficulty following simple instructions."

"Both of them."

"I've seen only one, but I'm told the other twin, Robert, behaves very similarly."

"It really fits quite nicely." Joseph smiled.

"You see something, don't you?"

"Something remarkable and wonderful. These are not twins, Christine. These are not two separate men born to the same mother at the same time with the same genetic history. These two gifted creatures are halves of one whole person whose development went awry, for reasons only God can explain. When they're together, they function as near to a whole as they are able. When they're apart, they scarcely function at all.''

"I don't quite follow you."

"They need each other the way your heart needs your brain, the way each part of your body needs every other part to function fully. Without each other, the twins merely survive. They breathe, they eat, they digest food. With each other, the organism is complete. It works. Together they are a savant.''

I took a moment to see the picture she was drawing, two beings whose sum was a thousand times more than its parts. It was a wild, almost crazy theory, proposed by the sanest human being I had ever known. "You mean that if the police had questioned them together—"

"Which they would never have done."

"—they would have told the truth."

"Quite possibly. If they were there to see what happened.''

"And if they weren't," I said, filling in the theoretical gaps, "they would at least know who it was who came into the apartment that day."

"Very likely."

My head was suddenly buzzing with possibilities. "Then the key to all this is to bring them together."

"It may be too late, you know. The organism may have atrophied.''

"It can't be." I looked across the table at her sheet of paper with its odd notations. It still made no sense to me, but what she had said did. "It's all there, Joseph, everything that ever happened to them, stored away in their minds, and if you're right, all we need to get it out is that key, putting them together."

"What will you do?"

I glanced at my watch. "I'll call Mrs. McAlpin as soon as I get home and see if she can work something out. And then I want to see if there was any time after the police arrived at that apartment when the twins were together."

"You will let me know how it all works out."

"Oh, yes." I stood and walked around the table to where she stood. "The moment I know. I'll come back and tell you."

"Good. That will mean a great deal to me."

I knew she was right. A good theory explains all the known facts and can be used to predict future occurrences. The twins had performed their "tricks," as Joseph put it, the morning of Good Friday when they were together with Magda. When Magda arrived at the Talley apartment and found Mrs. Talley dead, *she put one twin in the bedroom* so she could think about what to do. And when the police came, they naturally kept them apart for the reason Joseph had assumed. They'd have to be crazy to allow two suspected murderers to be together, giving them the opportunity to get their story straight.

All the way home to Oakwood, I turned Joseph's theory over and over, finding no flaws and seeing only great promise. When I turned into my driveway an hour or so later, I noticed something on my front doorstep, and after I parked the car, I walked around to the front door to see what it was. To my surprise and delight, it was a small peach tree, balled and bagged, with a note. I opened the door, brought the tree inside, and read: "We've knocked on your door a hundred times, but you're always out. Welcome to Oakwood. The McGuires (606) Midge, Don, Bobby, and Teri."

Number 606 was next door to the left, facing my house. I took the tree and put it outside my back door. The burlap bag felt damp, so I guessed I'd be able to leave it there long enough to make some phone calls, one of them to the McGuires.

My first call was to Greenwillow. Virginia McAlpin was, of course, not there, but I persuaded the person who answered to give me her home number. I dialed, and she picked up the phone.

"Virginia," I said, abandoning stuffy formality, "this is Chris Bennett. I have something to tell you."

I went on to describe Joseph's theory. Then I said, "It's

very important to get the twins together. Can you arrange for me to bring Robert to Greenwillow?''

''I don't see why not,'' she said. ''The release didn't contain any restrictions. I'll call my counterpart in Buffalo tomorrow. How soon would you be able to go?''

''I'll pack a bag and have it waiting.''

''This is really quite amazing, isn't it? I should think Dr. Sanderson would be most interested.''

''Let's not call in the medical community quite yet,'' I said. ''We don't know anything for certain, and our first priority is to find out who killed Mrs. Talley.''

''You're right. We'll keep this quiet till we've taken care of our immediate concern.''

I hoped she meant it. The last thing the Talley twins and I needed was to be descended upon by a gaggle of psychiatrists.

Naturally, I wanted to call Jack. I couldn't, because it was Sunday and I didn't have his home number. But even if I had, I wonder if I would have used it. Our relationship had changed last night from mostly business to the man-woman kind, and the change had made me hesitant about calling, even on a business matter.

So I called the McGuires and thanked them for the tree and accepted their invitation to Sunday supper at six, about half an hour from now.

But first, I had a very pleasurable job to do. I changed into sneakers, found a spade and a bag half-full of 5-10-5 fertilizer in the garage, and picked a place in the backyard where my little tree would eat up the sun.

It took most of my half hour to get the hole dug, the fertilizer added, the tree in and watered. When I had more time I would find two nice stakes and tie it up.

I stood back and admired my work. A line from one of my many volumes of poetry came back to me: ''The ripest peach is highest on the tree.'' Well, for a while at least I could reach anywhere they grew. Next year maybe I'd learn how to bake a peach pie.

20

Jack called Monday morning, sparing me an awkward moment. I told him I had gone upstate the previous day and spoken to an old friend who had offered the theory of the twins as halves of one whole. He said it certainly warranted testing, although he didn't sound as enthusiastic as I had hoped. I don't think he has the same philosophic bent that those of us immersed in English literature have.

"I'd like to find out if anyone at all ever spoke to the twins together," I said. "You know, like the police, the lawyers, the psychiatrist."

"I can tell you the police didn't. The last thing you'd ever do with suspects is put them together. Chances are the others saw them separately, too. But I guess you're looking for names."

"I guess I am," I said apologetically.

"Let me see what I can dig up. There's a fair chance the lawyer's still around if they got an 18B lawyer who works at a fixed fee after Legal Aid does the groundwork. They're often young, liberal guys with some experience. The psychiatrist may be tougher."

"I'll take what I can get."

"Stick around your phone this morning. I may have something after I get down to the house."

"Okay."

"I had a great time Saturday." He didn't sound business-like anymore.

"So did I."

"We'll do it again."

127

"I hope so."

"Good." He sounded happy.

Jack got back to me before eleven.

"There were two lawyers, both Legal Aid staff. One was Vincent Capozzo." He spelled it. "I can't find him listed anywhere. The lawyer for James was Arnold Gold, and I've been through both the yellow and white pages, and there are three Arnold Golds in practice in Manhattan and two in Brooklyn. Want the numbers?"

"I guess so." I wrote "Arnold Gold" on a piece of paper and listed the numbers. "I'll try them all," I said when he'd given me the last one.

"The psychiatrist was named H-O-C-H-W-A-L-D. I can't tell you much else about him."

"I checked my notes from my interview with O'Connor. He said they got someone from Kings County. What's that?"

"The big medical center in Brooklyn. I guess that's a place to start."

"Okay. I think I'll use the phone till I come up with something."

"I've got to go now. Talk to you later."

I started with the Brooklyn Arnold Golds. The first one's secretary said he had been in practice only since 1963 and he'd never been a Legal Aid lawyer. The second one's secretary tittered when I said 1950. She said her husband had just graduated from law school two years ago and hadn't been born until 1964. I gathered her husband was Arnold Gold.

I crossed off that one and called the first on my Manhattan list. The secretary there was kind enough to go and ask her Mr. Gold if he had had anything to do with the Talley case, but she, too, came back with a negative.

"Mr. Gold was admitted to the bar in 1958," she said. "But there's another Arnold Gold in Manhattan who's a little older, and I know he was a Legal Aid attorney at one time. Would you like his number?"

"Please."

She dictated the last number Jack had given me. I thanked her and dialed that one next.

That Mr. Gold was in court this morning, but his secretary admitted he was in his late sixties, and she told me rather proudly that he did a great deal of *pro bono* work. At the moment, he was involved in a class-action suit on behalf of the homeless.

I felt cheered by the details and more cheered by her promise that he would call me after three o'clock. In the intervening time I dashed over to Greenwillow and took Gene out for a drive. When we got back, I sat with James Talley, reminding him who I was and telling him, in answer to his questions, that I was still looking for his brother.

Arnold Gold was as good as his word. He called a little before four and said, yes, he had represented James Talley in 1950 when James was judged incompetent to stand trial. James had refused to cooperate in his own defense.

"In what way?" I asked, just to get it on my record.

"He didn't answer my questions. In fact—and I remember the case pretty well—he didn't talk to me at all even though I promised to keep everything secret."

"Did he tell you his name?"

"His name, yes. But very little beyond that. He asked for his brother incessantly and also for his mother."

"Did you ever bring the twins together?"

"That's against regulations," Arnold Gold said. "I never saw the brother."

"Did you have an opinion on James's guilt or innocence?"

"Frankly, no. There was a lot of evidence indicating one or both of the twins may have killed the mother, and no evidence to show that anyone else might have. I did the best for him that I could. It was one of my first cases, and I was glad to keep it from going to trial. It wouldn't have been an easy case to defend, at least with the resources I had at that time."

"Did anyone ever tell you that one of the twins' overcoats was missing from the coat closet?"

"What are you saying?" the lawyer asked crisply.

"The girl who found the body on Easter Sunday morning stayed the day. When the twins were being taken into custody, she found only one overcoat in the closet, and the clothes were pushed apart as though someone had been looking for something specific."

"To put on and cover up what he was wearing."

"That's the way I see it," I said.

"There was certainly no mention of anything missing in the police file. In fact, if memory serves, the record showed that nothing in the apartment had been taken."

"It does show that. I've been through most of it."

"Are you telling me the police withheld information?"

"It's possible," I said.

"You have evidence to that effect?"

"I've spoken to the girl—she's in her late fifties now—and she swears she told the police when she saw the coat missing and later called and left a message. I've also talked to the detective's partner, the man who took some notes and statements at the scene. He remembers both her calling attention to the missing coat and leaving a message. The detective actually assigned to the case doesn't recall anything."

"He wouldn't," the lawyer said derisively, and muttered something unintelligible that I was relieved not to hear distinctly. "Are they prepared to testify to that effect?"

I smiled. Despite his age, he was certainly an eager beaver. "I don't know, and I don't know if it's necessary. If I find out anything substantive, would you like me to call you?"

"I certainly would."

"I have one more question, Mr. Gold. What would have happened to any money Mrs. Talley had when she died?"

"Depends on whether she had a will. If she died intestate, one third would have gone to her husband and two thirds to her children. In practice, all three of them would have inherited a third."

"The twins could inherit even though they were guilty of murder?"

"They weren't guilty. They never stood trial and they were

never convicted. You can check the surrogate courts in Brooklyn to see the disposition of her estate. I had nothing to do with that.''

I thanked him and promised to get back to him if I learned anything new. I had a feeling he was champing at the bit to get back to James Talley's defense, this time with a lifetime of experience to back him up.

That evening Melanie Gross called and invited me over. They had heard from the law student cousin who had researched Mrs. Talley's estate in Brooklyn. Mrs. Talley had indeed died intestate, but what was most surprising was the amount of money she had left. Mrs. Talley had apparently been a rather wealthy woman in her own right, whether her husband knew it or not. She left approximately $350,000 in savings accounts, blue-chip stocks, and United States Treasuries. The interest alone on that amount of money was more than the average income in 1950. She could well have afforded to pay Magda a dollar an hour, to own a fur coat, to live a comfortable life.

According to the surrogate's records, the money was divided in thirds, just as Arnold Gold had described. The twins' money was held in trust and administered by a court-appointed lawyer. With the twins institutionalized for forty years, I suspected the money had grown immensely.

But Patrick Talley had inherited a third of that amount, a staggering sum for a man supporting two families for over fourteen years. It provided a reason why he might not have wanted to divorce Alberta and thereby disinherit himself, and a reason, in addition to not having to pay alimony, to want her dead. I remembered that Kathleen Mackey had started to say something when her brother cut her off, and I wondered whether it had to do with her father inheriting this money. With over a hundred thousand dollars, he could easily have paid for a big house in 1950, when real estate values were far below what they are today.

While I was at the Grosses', Melanie's uncle called with

a report on the Talley house on Grand Bahama Island. Mel returned from the kitchen sporting a broad smile.

"Wait till you hear this," she said, taking her seat in the family room near the empty fireplace. "That address you gave me? My uncle says it's a whole neighborhood of mansions. *Mansions!* And if my uncle says so, you can believe it."

"So the Talleys ended up rich," I said.

"Surprised?" Mel asked.

"Not at all. Everything's been pointing towards it."

"So where do you go from here?"

"I really don't know. I'm waiting to hear from Virginia McAlpin. The sooner we get the twins together, the better chance we have of solving this thing."

Virginia called when I got home. She had been trying me on and off and not finding me in. The group home in Buffalo had no problem about releasing Robert, whom they described as docile and manageable. They wanted a day to prepare him. Anytime starting with the Fourth would be fine. I told her I would fly up as soon as I got a reservation.

I got myself on a plane the morning of the Fourth of July. I was getting ready for bed when the phone rang. It was Jack.

I briefed him on all that was new, and then he gave me some news.

"I ran Paul Antonetti's name today," he said. "I even checked with the FBI. There's no indication he was ever in trouble after that day in 1950."

"Sounds like you think he just stopped being a suspect."

"I think it's less likely. I also think that to question someone forty years after the only mistake he ever made puts him in a pretty awkward position."

"Agreed."

"So let's hold on to his name and use it if we get stuck."

I laughed. "Jack, I'm stuck now. If the twins don't come up with something, I don't know where to go from here. If Patrick Talley didn't do it, I don't know who did, and I don't know how to prove that Patrick did."

"Well, if your idea about the twins works, it's a cinch they'll ID their own father."

"I hope so." I wasn't as sure as he was. I didn't know when Patrick had left his first family. If it was when the twins were babies, they'd have no idea who he was, savants or not.

"You're flying up to Buffalo Wednesday."

"First thing in the morning. I'll take a cab to the home, have lunch there, and take Robert back."

"Will you give me a call when you get back?"

"Sure."

He gave me his home phone number. "I'm working on the Fourth myself. How about I come up on Saturday to see your twins in action? We can have something to eat afterward. Not too formal. It's getting pretty hot and I hate to wear a tie."

I told him I'd like that, and we hung up. It was quite late and I was really tired.

21

One thing I have never worried about is taxes. Lots of other people worry, but when you turn over virtually everything you earn to a convent, taxes don't loom very important on your horizon. But I know that acquiring tax-free income is very desirable, and I also know that the Bahamas are known as a haven for folks with money whose origins are murky.

So I got up Tuesday morning trying to figure out what Patrick Talley might have done to come into the amount and kind of money that would draw him to a tax haven.

The money he had inherited from Alberta came through legal channels and would have been taxed according to the laws of the time. I wondered about real estate deals. I had heard of people coming to closings with briefcases—or paper bags—full of cash. But how do you check up on that kind of thing forty years after the fact?

Patrick Talley had been part of a small group of independent insurance agents that was still listed in the phone book. I decided to drive over and see if they could dig up any old records on him.

The company's office was in northern New Jersey, not too far from the house the Talleys bought after Alberta died. I crossed the Tappan Zee Bridge and was there by nine-thirty.

It was a newish yellow brick building, and there was a kind of casual air among the partners and employees that probably made it fun to work for. The men sat at their desks in shirt-sleeves, and the women wore summery dresses and sandals with bare legs.

It took me a while to get to see someone who might be in a position to help me, Mr. Rasmussen, a graying man with very blue eyes. I went through my story of researching the unsolved death of Mr. Talley's first wife, and he assured me he had known Pat in the fifties—''when I was a lot younger than I am now''—and that his father had worked with Pat.

I asked some questions and got a lot of anecdotes in return. Either he didn't take me seriously or this was his technique for putting me off.

He confirmed what Patrick Jr. had said, that Pat had continued working past normal retirement, taking only a few clients. Eventually, he and his wife—''his second wife, I think it was''—had moved to a little farm somewhere. It amused me that the bungalow had become a farm. Rasmussen didn't seem to know where the farm was, but he remembered when Pat died; he'd been to the funeral. ''Lots of people,'' he said. ''Pat was really loved.''

So I knew he was lying, but I didn't know why or about what. I couldn't ask him about Patrick Talley's whereabouts on Good Friday 1950, because Rasmussen had probably been a teenager then and not yet involved with the business.

Eventually I just gave up. I couldn't stay all day, and I

couldn't crack the protective shell he had built around the Patrick Talley story. Finally I said, "Well, if you think of anything, please give me a call." I said my name and number loudly enough that the other shirt-sleeves in the area could hear and then I wrote my name, address, and number on a sheet of his paper.

On the way home, I stopped in my bank and took out enough cash to pay for one round trip to Buffalo and one one-way back.

My last ploy at the insurance company paid off that evening. The phone rang, and when I answered, a man said, "Christine Bennett?"

"Yes, it is."

"You the one wants to know about Pat Talley?"

"That's right."

"Why?"

I decided to be frank. "I think there's something funny about his finances."

"Ya damned right. That was no farm he bought."

"I know that."

"Ever hear of Mayfair Fuels?"

"No." I grabbed a pencil and started writing.

"Biggest fire they ever had in New Jersey."

"When was it?" I asked.

" 'Bout fifty-nine."

"Did he insure them?"

"Well, someone named Pat Talley did."

"Was it arson?" I asked boldly.

"Suspicious. Nothing was ever proved. Three-million-dollar payoff."

"That's a lot of money."

"Mayfair never rebuilt."

"I see."

"Town was against it, neighbors were against it. They made it look like they wanted to. 'F you ask me, they took their share and ran."

He couldn't have made it clearer if he'd spelled it out. "I appreciate your calling."

"Just thought I'd set the record straight." He hung up.

I looked down at what I'd scribbled: They took their share and ran. And the other share, I thought—had it ended up in the Bahamas?

22

The cab dropped me off at the entrance to a building that could have been an old school. It was in a suburb of Buffalo, nearer the airport than the city, so I never got to see the city at all.

A young woman named Carolyn Donatera was waiting for me, checked my identification, and greeted me warmly.

"I've told Robert you're coming, but his memory span isn't very good and it's likely he won't have any idea who you are. But he reacted very positively when I told him he would see his brother."

She took me to his room. He was sitting at a large window, looking out at the people in the yard. When he turned his head to look at me I had to tell myself this was really a different person from the one I had left behind. Robert was as identical to James as I have ever seen among twins. I introduced myself and went to where he was sitting and shook his hand. He looked at me as James had that first time, searchingly. "I want my brother," he said in a voice indistinguishable from James's.

"I'm going to take you to see him, Robert. Tonight we'll see James."

"My brother?"

"Yes." I pulled out a snapshot Virginia McAlpin had given me.

Robert studied it. "My brother," he said. He held the photo, entranced by it.

"That's right. That's James."

Carolyn guided me away from him. "Will you be able to handle him all right?"

"My cousin has been retarded from birth, and he was my first friend. I don't think Robert will give me any trouble."

We had lunch together in the dining room and then Carolyn said she would drive us to the airport. Robert's clothes had been packed in two suitcases, which we checked through to LaGuardia. After Carolyn left us, I talked quietly to Robert, wondering how much, if anything, of what I said remained with him. I wanted to assure him that I would be there for the whole trip, comforting this child of a man who may not have needed comforting and may have needed more than I gave. My cousin Gene is very responsive. You know immediately that something is right or wrong. The Talley twins, by contrast, were opaque.

The flight was smooth. Robert drank a glass of orange juice and looked out the window. At the airport we managed to get the luggage to the covered garage where I had parked to be close, and then I drove north.

Virginia had ducked out of her family picnic to be at Greenwillow when we arrived. I really loved the way she greeted Robert; she was a marvelous person to run the home. Aunt Meg had made a good decision.

We went up the steps and down the hall to James's room. Virginia had seen to it that he would be waiting alone for his precious moment. I must admit that my nerves were frazzled as we reached the door.

Virginia knocked and opened the door. James was sitting in his easy chair, looking at nothing in particular. I noticed that a second similar chair had been moved into the room.

"James," Virginia said, "here's Robert."

I was the one who nearly cried. James turned and looked at his brother. Then he stood up. Robert walked toward him stopping a few paces away from him. It occurred to me that they might not recognize each other because they had last seen each other as young men, not as people entering old age. But neither seemed surprised and neither said a word. They just stared.

And then, slowly, I saw James's mouth loosen into a smile. His eyes, which often seemed so vacant, were now inhabited. Although Robert's back was toward me, I had no doubt but that his face reflected his brother's.

They did not touch each other. I touched Virginia, reaching my hand to find her arm as my eyes filled with tears. We backed away, I feeling more like an intruder than I had ever felt before.

I saw James nod his head slightly. Then he sat in his chair, and Robert found and sat in the other. James was now smiling broadly. In the few minutes the brothers had shared the room, James had become a person.

I felt deeply conflicted. I wanted to observe the reconciliation, but I wanted also to leave the men alone. Virginia took charge of the situation.

She walked nearer to the twins and said, "Would you gentlemen like to have dinner here in the room?"

Robert said, "Dinner," and James said, "I'm hungry."

"Good. Chris and I will bring up some trays."

We went downstairs together. "I've got to get back to my family," Virginia said. "You're staying, aren't you?"

"If you don't mind."

"I hoped you'd stay. Just follow your instincts. Someone's coming over later to put a second bed in James's room. I think they should be together as much as they want."

"I agree."

We had reached the kitchen, where preparations for dinner were nearly done. Virginia asked for three trays. When they had been made up, one of the residents carried the third one upstairs for us. We arranged them on James's table, and then Virginia left.

The twins sat opposite each other, and I sat on the side between. "I'm Chris," I said.

"I'm Robert."

"I'm James."

"I brought you here on an airplane today," I said to Robert. "Do you remember that?"

He smiled at me and shook his head.

"This place is called Greenwillow."

Each of them repeated it.

"Do you remember my name?" I asked.

"Chris," they chorused.

"That's right. Chris Bennett. My cousin Gene lives here at Greenwillow. I come here a lot to visit him. I'll visit you a lot, too. I'd like to be friends with you."

The dinner was hamburgers and french fries, a can of Coke, and vanilla ice cream, an all-American meal to celebrate our country's birthday.

"Do you like hamburgers?" I asked.

"I like mine with ketchup," James said.

"Here's some ketchup." I picked up the sealed packet that was on his tray and tore it open. "You can squeeze it on," I explained, showing him.

"Where's the bottle?"

"The bottle's in the kitchen. It's easier to use these on a tray."

"I like that," Robert said. He had managed to open his ketchup packet himself with only slight damage. He wiped up the spilled red sauce with his napkin.

"This is a good Fourth of July dinner," I said. "You know that today is the Fourth of July, don't you?" I addressed the question to both of them.

"No, it's not," Robert answered. He didn't seem upset at my error. He was smiling.

"Sure it is. It's Wednesday, July fourth."

"Today is April ninth," James said. "It's Easter Sunday."

23

My thought at that moment was, I wish Joseph were here. It would have been wonderful for her to see firsthand how right she was. Forty years of their lives had been lost, and the only saving grace was that the twins had forgotten—or never comprehended—how bad those years had been.

I explained simply that they had been apart for a long time. I promised to bring a calendar the next day and we would talk about it. I stayed until the second bed was put in the room. Then I left them in the care of Greenwillow.

Thursday morning I drove to Greenwillow as early as I felt was decent, carrying a church calendar Aunt Meg kept in the kitchen. The twins were sitting jacketless in the backyard. I pulled a chair over and said good morning.

"Good morning, Chris." James.

"Good morning, Chris." Robert.

"It's a nice day, isn't it?"

"Warm," James said.

"When were you born, James?"

"February nineteenth, 1921."

"I was born first," Robert added. "He's the baby."

"What day of the week was that?"

"Saturday," they chorused.

I took a sheet of paper from my bag on which I had jotted down some dates and days, using Aunt Meg's old almanac. "Do you remember May sixteenth, 1949?"

"I remember," Robert said. "It was a Monday."

"It was sunny," James said. "Magda came and we went out for a walk."

"Did she come in the morning or the afternoon?"

"In the afternoon. In May she always came in the afternoon."

That would fit with what I knew. Magda was still in high school then. It wasn't until the following fall that she started coming in the morning.

"What day would July fifth, 1990, be?" I asked.

They looked thoughtful.

"Thursday," James said.

"Yes," I agreed. "It would be Thursday. Robert, James." I looked at each of them. "One day in 1950, someone put you in one place and you in another place. Yesterday you came back together. This is 1990." I opened Aunt Meg's calendar and turned the pages until I got to July. I put my finger on the fifth.

"Where is 1950?" Robert asked.

"It's gone," I said. Ridiculously, I wanted to apologize, to say how sorry I was that I couldn't get it back for them.

They had become contemplative, if that was the word. Perhaps they were trying to assimilate what I had said. I sat quietly, not wanting to complicate their thoughts with something else new.

Finally James said, "Nineteen fifty-one."

After a moment, Robert said, "Nineteen fifty-two."

They alternated the years until Robert reached 1990. Then they stopped. They had brought themselves up-to-date.

I hung around Greenwillow most of the day, but I spent only a little time now and then with the twins. I visited with Gene, went out to lunch, chatted with Virginia. Each time I returned to the twins, they greeted me like a long-lost friend.

I played the calendar game with them again, asking what day of the week dates before and after their lifetime occurred on. They seemed to alternate in giving answers without ever overtly agreeing to do so, and they were always correct.

In the afternoon I walked with them in the small area

behind the residence. "Do you remember Dr. Weintraub?"
I asked.

"Oh yes," James responded. "He plays games with us."

"What kind of games?"

"Number games," Robert said, and I recalled the twins'
talent for coming up with prime numbers of increasingly
larger denomination.

"When was the last time you saw him?"

"Friday," James said, and my heart skipped a beat.
"March thirty-first. He came after lunch. We played the radio game with him."

"What's the radio game?"

"President Truman broke away from reporters during his
morning constitutional to talk to a young lady in a wheel-
chair. The lady, Miss Sue Ann Rogers from Iowa City, said
afterward that she just wanted to tell the president how proud
she was of him and how happy she was to have shaken his
hand. Reporters who stopped to speak to Miss Rogers were
unable to catch up with the president and returned instead to
the White House." Robert spoke these words with the tone
and cadence of a seasoned, old-time radio announcer, and I
realized he was repeating something he had heard on the
radio.

"That's a good game," I said. "What did Dr. Weintraub
say when you told him that?"

"Good for you, Robert," James said. "You're a man of
many talents."

"You both are," I told them, wondering later if they had
any idea what the sentence meant. But it didn't seem to matter to the twins; they were happy.

When I got home I found a large, thick envelope on the
doormat. The return address was New Hope, James's erst-
while home. I opened the envelope and found a number of
stapled scientific papers, all printed on one side, and a brief
note from Dr. Sanderson apologizing for the lateness of the
package.

It seemed to me there was very little I could learn from

the material that would help me to find Mrs. Talley's murderer, but I thought it would be interesting to see the kinds of experiments that had been done with the twins. And I was particularly interested in Dr. Weintraub's letter setting forth his reasons for believing in the twins' innocence.

The letter turned out to be at the top of the pile, and I pulled it out of the rubber-banded pack and took it to the dining room. It was a beautifully written document in which the doctor described the twins, whom he had known over a period of nearly two years, in terms that would have deflated the toughest prosecutor. He had visited each of the twins in jail (separately, I noted), and had been shocked at the degree of regression each exhibited.

Finally there was an impassioned plea for a reexamination of the facts of the case, the immediate release on bond of the twins to the custody of an institution he named, and a new effort to find the killer of Mrs. Talley.

Jack called as I finished reading the letter. This time his enthusiasm was as great as his amazement. "You really did it," he said after I'd run through yesterday and today. "Did you ask them anything about Good Friday?"

"Not yet. I'm waiting for you to be there. I really don't know what to do if they name someone as the killer."

"I'll bring a tape recorder. Can I pick you up about ten?"

"Ten's fine."

After we hung up, I called Magda and told her the news.

"My boys are together," she said, sounding tearful.

"I'd like you to see them. Are you free tomorrow?"

"Yes. I can be free."

"I'll pick you up and we'll drive to Greenwillow together."

She agreed to be ready at nine-thirty. I was starting to worry about my car. It was seeing more activity in two weeks than in all the years I'd owned it.

24

The twins didn't really recognize her until she spoke.

"My boys," she said, looking from one to the other. "It's me, Magda. Look at you, how wonderful you look."

They broke into smiles, and I sat on a chair a little away from them to keep out of the conversation. I had told Magda not to talk to them about Good Friday. Instead, she reviewed days she had spent with them, remembering with delight skirts, sweaters, and dresses she had worn in the 1950s when Robert and James described them.

At one point Magda tried to ask them about a date during their forty-year hiatus. The reaction was striking. They looked at each other but said nothing. There was no little smile, no brightening eyes, just the silence of life without memory.

I joined them after a while and asked them if they remembered going to church. Working backward from April 1950, they gave me dates three or four weeks apart, details—"Mama wore her fur coat"—and occasionally some special thing that happened—"A baby cried." At one point I asked them if they remembered the mass, and to my amazement, they began to recite in Latin.

"Dominus vobiscum." James.

"Et cum spiritu tuo." Robert.

"Sursum corda." James.

"Habemus ad Dominum." Robert.

"Gratias agamus Domino Deo nostro." James.

"Dignum et justum est." Robert.

It gave me a rather wonderful feeling of having entered a

time warp. I have no memory of Latin masses, which ended with John XXIII.

I took Magda home early enough that I would avoid the commuter rush when I returned to Oakwood. In and out of New York twice in one day is a little more than I find tolerable.

I ate dinner with Dr. Sanderson's pile of papers next to me. Besides developing a great respect for Dr. Weintraub, I felt he must have been a very warm and caring man. His affection for the twins crept into his writing. I found it refreshing.

The phone rang while I was getting ready for bed.

"Christine Bennett?" a man asked.

"That's right."

"This is Harry Forrest. I live on Sunset Drive, over on the other side of town. How're you doing with those twins?"

"Just fine. I'm working hard at it."

"Got anything yet or are you still digging?"

For some reason, he irritated me. "I'm still trying, Mr. Forrest."

"Well, good luck. Just wanted to know how things were going."

That night, for the first time since I had left St. Stephen's, I had trouble falling asleep. Tomorrow we would ask the twins the crucial questions of that long-ago Good Friday. It would surely be an emotional day.

And for me, too, it would be special. It was a week since I had seen Jack, and I found myself wanting him in a very physical way. I wanted to be near him. I wanted to touch him. I dearly wanted to be kissed.

So I tossed and turned for a while, anticipating the coming day.

Jack arrived a little before ten, armed with a small tape recorder, several tapes, and fresh batteries. We drove in his car and arrived at Greenwillow at ten-thirty.

Virginia didn't ordinarily work on weekends, and as she didn't know of my plans for today, she was absent. The twins were sitting at a round, umbrellaed table behind the building, where we'd been doing our talking since the Fourth. I stopped and said hello to Gene, introducing him to Jack. I told Gene we'd have lunch with him later, and he went to join a friend. Gene happens to love Greenwillow. Sometimes on my visits I've had the feeling he'd rather be with another resident than with me.

We joined the twins at their table, and I introduced Jack. He showed them the tape recorder and let each of them say something which he played back. They were fascinated by the sound of their voices, and they agreed on tape to let Jack record our conversation. We began by demonstrating their calendar talents and then I asked them if they remembered April seventh, 1950.

There was no hesitation. They recalled the doorbell ringing and Magda coming in. They recounted their departure to the park, Magda's questions about the day she was born, their answers. As I listened, I realized Magda had been my second-best witness; everything she had said was corroborated by the twins.

We relived their return to the apartment, Mama's return with two bags of groceries—"Mama bought Corn Flakes today," from James—and Magda's departure.

"Did you eat lunch?" I asked.

"Cheese sandwiches," Robert said. "There's no ham today. It's Good Friday." (I could almost hear his mother explaining it to him.)

After lunch, Mama turned on the radio and sat down with a book. "You boys go to your bedroom and be good boys." James said the words as though he were his own mother.

They went to their bedroom and looked at pictures in a magazine. (It sounded like *Life*, but I couldn't be sure).

There was silence. I could imagine their minds turning the pages of the forty-year-old magazine.

Jack signaled that he wanted to change the tape, and I waited till he had the new one going.

"Did someone come to visit?" I asked.

"The doorbell," Robert said.

"Did Mama answer the door?"

"Mama." James.

"Who was there?"

"Jerry," Robert said.

"Jerry," I echoed. "Who's Jerry?"

Silence. One of the questions they can't answer. Over and over I realized they were little more than recording machines. Substantive questions left them nonplussed.

"What is Jerry's last name?"

Silence.

"Did Jerry visit you before April seventh?"

They did their staring bit. "March twenty-third," James said. "It was raining."

"Did you talk to Jerry on March twenty-third?"

"We played games," Robert said. "Jerry brought chocolate."

"Is Jerry your friend?"

"Jerry is my friend." James.

"Do you like him?"

"I like him." Robert. "Jerry is my friend."

"Is Jerry a little boy or a big man?"

"Jerry is a big man." James.

"Does Jerry live in your building?"

Silence.

"Did you play number games with Jerry?"

"No." Robert.

"Did you play the radio game?"

They thought for a moment. "We played the radio game on January seventeenth," James said. "Jerry's shoes had snow. Mama said, 'Wipe your feet before you come in.' "

I gave it one more try. "What games did you play with Jerry?"

"The match game." Robert.

"Did you make fires?" I asked.

Silence.

"Hold on," Jack said. "I'll be right back."

He went into the building, and I turned off the tape recorder. It was getting very hot and I wondered whether we should adjourn to the twins' room, but I hated to break the continuity.

Jack came back with a box of toothpicks. "Can you play the match game with these?"

Robert took the box and dumped it on the table. Toothpicks rolled around and came to a stop. The twins looked at the scattered toothpicks, then at each other.

"Seventy-nine," James said.

"I don't believe what I'm seeing," Jack said. He put the toothpicks back in the box by twos. At the end, one was left. "Seventy-nine," he said. "Goddamn."

"That's the match game," I said to the twins.

They nodded.

I switched the tape recorder on. "You played the match game with Jerry, and once you played the radio game. And you played . . ." I left it open.

"The hiding game," Robert completed my sentence.

"Hide-and-seek," I interpreted. "No wonder there was so much noise in that apartment." I paused. "Jerry came to visit you on April seventh. Mama opened the door. What did Jerry say?"

"Some day, isn't it?" James.

"Just beautiful. I was out this morning." Robert.

"You look nice. I like your hair." James.

"Oh, thank you. I had it done. For the holidays. Would you like some tea, Jerry?" Robert.

"Sure." James.

"I got some nice Danish at the bakery." Robert.

Something started working at my brain. A boyfriend? Did Alberta Talley have a boyfriend?

"Where are the boys?" James.

"In their room looking at magazines." Robert.

"I want to talk to you about them." James.

"I know you do, but I gave you my answer. There's just the three of us now, and it's best for us to stay together." Robert.

"It wouldn't be for long, a week, maybe two." James.

"I told you no, Jerry. I wish you'd listen to me. I'm not about to change my mind." Robert.

"It's important. It's really important. They'll be well taken care of. I give you my word." James.

"And I gave you my last word. Now, do you want to be nice and have a cup of tea or do you want to leave?" Robert.

"I just can't take no for an answer." James.

"Well, you'll have to." Robert.

"This is my life we're talking about," James said in a loud voice.

"Get out of here, Jerry." Robert.

"Not until you say I can have them." James.

"What are you doing with that?" Robert.

"Come on, Mrs. T. Give a little, will you?" James.

"Get out of here, Jerry." Robert's voice rose with fear and panic. "Get away from me!"

James let out a sound of pain.

Then Robert said, "There's the witch."

"What witch?" I asked, feeling confused.

"The witch with the broom. The witch down there." He pointed toward the ground.

"Selma Franklin," I breathed. "She must have been pounding on the ceiling. *She was home, Jack.*"

"They probably turned over some chairs in the scuffle," Jack said.

"Were you boys still in your room?" I asked.

They nodded.

"After you heard the witch, what happened?"

Robert screamed, a shrill, bloodcurdling sound. I jumped, startled, and noticed people rushing toward us. I got up and waved them away. I didn't blame them. It had sounded as though he were being killed.

The thought made me feel a little sick. It was his mother who was being killed, right here, right now, forty years ago.

"Robert! James! Help me! Oh, help me." Robert started to cry. I put my hand on his shoulder. "Mama," he whimpered, and I wondered if he was replaying himself or feeling the pain all over again, or both.

"Mama," James echoed.

"Oh Christ, oh Christ." Robert.

"There's the doorbell," James said, cocking his head as though he heard it again.

"Shhh." Robert.

"There's the doorbell." James.

"Selma Franklin," I whispered.

There was silence at our table as we all waited tensely for her to go away. Both the twins were crying as quietly as they could so as not to anger Jerry.

"Robert, go into your mother's room and close the door. Quick." Robert.

I could hear the tape running and twins sniffling.

"That's it," Jack said. "He separated them."

"You're right. That's all they'll remember till Robert comes out of the bedroom."

Jack flicked off the tape recorder. "Let's take a breather. This has been pretty exhausting."

I reached over to lay an arm on each twin's shoulder. "It's okay," I comforted them. I found some tissues in my bag and gave one to each of them.

I noticed the Greenwillow group moving toward the building, and I realized it was time for lunch. Gene was coming toward us. I had promised him lunch, and although I regretted having to leave the twins, I knew better than to disappoint Gene.

We went inside, and I left the twins in the care of a staff member. Then the three of us went out to Jack's car.

Gene wanted a hamburger and shake, and after we were seated, Jack excused himself. When he came back, he told Gene he had to talk to me for a minute, if that was okay. Anything was okay with Gene if you were nice to him, and he didn't even look as though he was listening. The place mat on the tray had his attention.

"I just called the squad," Jack said. "Something about the name Jerry started me thinking. I don't know if there's anything to it, but Patrick Talley's middle name was Jerome."

"Jerry," I said. "It's possible, isn't it? She could have called him Jerry. Maybe he was named after his father and they called him by his middle name."

"Could be."

"But the people at the agency he worked at, they referred to him as Pat."

Jack shrugged. "They met him later in his life. Who knows?"

"It sounded to me like a boyfriend when the conversation started."

"It sure as hell wasn't a stranger."

"Whoever it was, he wanted to take the twins away from her. He also separated them as soon as they came on the scene. It's almost as though he knew he could stop them from recording the events."

"Patrick might know that. What about the psychiatrist?"

I shook my head. "I've been reading the papers about the twins. There's no hint Dr. Weintraub knew anything about that. And I think his first name was Morris. Besides, that was 1950, and she would have called him 'Doctor.' "

"Listen, Chris—"

"Kix," my cousin interjected. "That's Kix."

Jack turned to look at me. His look of surprise changed to something less readable. "Kix?"

I'm sure I turned beet red. "It's an old family name," I sputtered.

"It's great." He turned to Gene. "Thanks, Gene."

Gene smiled broadly. All you have to do is be nice to him and he's the sweetest person in the world. "She's Kix. She's not that brown lady anymore. She's Kix."

The "brown lady," of course, was me in my habit. Please, I signaled my cousin silently, let me be the one to tell him.

Jack took it all in stride, and we finished our lunch and went back to Greenwillow.

25

We sat in the lounge for a while to talk over what we had.

"If it was Patrick," I said, "then he left home when the twins were very small and he just came back as a kind of friend."

"I don't like it," Jack said. "There was a lot of bitterness in that split. Patrick Talley was no friend."

"Maybe Alberta had just inherited all that money and he wanted to make sure she wouldn't disinherit him."

"Possible."

"Well, it's not the gas man. And it doesn't sound like it's a neighbor. Suppose it was a boyfriend, Jack, someone who wanted to spend time with Alberta without the twins around."

"If that's the case, he's dead and gone, and we don't have much chance of finding out who he was."

"You know, I've really done what I set out to do. I've proved to myself that the twins didn't kill their mother. If I play that tape for the Oakwood council, I can't see how they can deny Greenwillow the variance."

"If you feel that way, we can take a swim in the Sound this afternoon."

It was a tempting thought on a hot day, but I knew I couldn't just drop the case. "Let's find out what happened after Robert came out of his mother's room."

Robert had come out for the simplest of reasons: he had to go to the bathroom. Once out, the twins tried to revive their dead mother, moving her, pulling the knife out of her body, talking to her. It was a pitiful tale, two very dependent children completely at a loss. My heart ached listening to them.

Finally, on Easter Sunday morning, Magda came to their rescue.

"The bell," James said.

"Did you answer the door?" I asked.

"No. Mama said, 'Don't answer the door, Robert.' "

" 'Don't answer the door, James.' "

"Who was at the door?"

"Magda came in." Robert.

They recounted the few things that happened before Magda separated them. And that, for all intents and purposes, was the end of their life as they knew it.

The one exception was the brief time they were together as they were getting ready to leave the apartment for the police station.

Magda gave James his coat and he put it on. Then, "Mr. O'Connor, Robert's coat is missing." Robert.

"What?" James.

"His coat is missing. Look in the closet. Somebody took it." Robert.

"Come on, honey, it's seven o'clock. Would you find something for him to put on so we can get out of here?" James.

"But maybe somebody took it." Robert.

"And maybe he left it somewhere. I don't have all night." James.

"Here, Robert, wear your raincoat. That's a good boy." Robert.

Downstairs, they were put into two police cars, and that was the end. Jack turned off the tape recorder.

"You were good boys," I said to the twins after a moment.

"Jerry was bad," James said.

"Yes, I think he was."

"The witch was bad," Robert said.

I felt very bad about the witch. I patted Robert's shoulder, but I didn't say anything. I still had a difficult task ahead of me.

* * *

By the time we left, it was late afternoon. It was too late for a swim, and anyway, that was kind of a problem for me. I wasn't used to baring quite so much of myself in public. But an Oakwood residents' association owned a piece of beach along a protected cove on the Long Island Sound, and I had inherited Aunt Meg's share along with the house. I hadn't visited it since moving in, but I remembered it as a lovely spot. We drove there, took our shoes off, and walked in the sand.

The beach, as usual, was almost empty. We walked around the half circle of the inlet, stopped for a while at the point, and came back. We had stopped talking by then. We were out of ideas. If it was Patrick, he was dead. If it was a boyfriend, he was dead. Surely we could no longer suspect Paul Antonetti or the mailman or Selma Franklin. I still wanted it to be Patrick, but it seemed less and less likely.

As we walked back along the beach, a woman in a bathing suit came over.

"Are you Christine Bennett?"

"Yes, I am."

"Hi. I'm Betsy Gore. I was at the council meeting last month. I want you to know I'm with you."

"Thank you very much."

"How are you doing?"

"Better than I hoped. I'm really making progress."

"Wonderful! If you need any help, we're in the book, G-O-R-E."

I thanked her and we resumed our walk. "That's the third one," I told Jack.

"Third what?"

"Third person who's talked to me about it since the meeting. The mayor called a week or so ago, and someone from town called last night."

"You're getting pretty popular. Pretty soon you'll be running for public office."

"Not a chance."

"Suppose we have dinner and think about something else for a while."

"Sounds good."

We got back to the house about eight-thirty. I had had a glass of wine with dinner and I was feeling relaxed. We had really fought off talking about the Talley murder, which was good for both of us. Our lives and our worlds held a lot of other interesting things, and we enjoyed exploring them.

Jack was thirsty, so we went to the kitchen and I got out some ice and a container of orange juice, but all he wanted was water. He drained the glass and set it on the counter.

"I pulled out a book of poetry after I saw you last week."

I felt touched. "I hope you liked it."

"I went back and looked at what those guys wrote three, four hundred years ago. Love and death over and over. Made me feel like very little had changed."

"Very little has."

That's when he took me in his arms. It didn't catch me off guard or surprise me in any way. I had known when we walked into the house. I felt I had been waiting for this moment since ten o'clock this morning, putting it on hold for all those hours that we were at Greenwillow, that we spent on the beach and having dinner. But I knew as we kissed that I had made a mistake in judgment; I had withheld something vital about myself, something he had a right to know if we were to continue seeing each other, which I dearly wanted.

"Come with me," I said softly as our kiss ended, as his hands began touching me more intimately, more passionately, then I could have imagined a month ago. "I have to tell you something."

"It can wait."

"No. Please. It's waited too long."

We went into the living room and sat on Aunt Meg's comfortable sofa, Jack's arm around me. I lifted his hand and kissed it.

"I was a nun until five weeks ago," I said.

He was quiet for so long that I knew he just couldn't think

of the right thing to say. There wasn't any right thing, and I wanted him to know that.

"That's what your cousin meant at lunch today," he said finally. "The brown lady."

"I was a Franciscan. We wore a brown habit. It was obligatory. I don't think Gene was ever sure I was the person underneath all those folds."

He touched my hair. "It's starting to grow back."

"A lot of things are starting to happen. I'll feel better if I tell you."

"I'm listening."

My mother died when I was fourteen. Because she was both loving and courageous, she arranged formally and informally that I would live with Aunt Meg, Uncle Will, and Gene if and when she died. I had known them all my life, and it was the best place I could think of being, except for my mother's home.

Perhaps because she had doubts or misgivings, she also planted certain seeds in me. She talked glowingly of the life of a nun. We visited St. Stephen's when I was only thirteen. It was like stepping into another world. It was so beautiful, so mystical—all those nuns in their brown habits walking from building to building, the novices with their heads down and their arms crossed and hands concealed in their sleeves. It seemed like the most wonderful life to me.

According to their rules, I couldn't enter till I was eighteen and had finished high school, but it didn't work out that way. Although my life with my aunt and uncle was as good as life could be without my mother, my presence in the house became a problem because of Gene.

My uncle and aunt had learned to cope with Gene's retardation; what was harder was the many physical problems that were visited on him. Sores popped up on his body; breathing difficulties sometimes hospitalized him for days at a time, leaving Meg and Will fearful for his life. When those times came, Aunt Meg would stay overnight with Gene, a practice that had been easy in the past. Now she was leaving a fourteen-year-old girl, whose mother had recently died, alone in the house, sometimes till Uncle Will returned late in the evening, sometimes overnight if Will was on the road. The anguish this caused her was something awful.

During the year I lived with them, we visited St. Stephen's twice, and I resolved to join the order. I tried to make myself into the kind of person they would want, devout and devoted.

What finally happened was that Gene was hospitalized again after my fifteenth birthday, and complications set it. Suddenly it looked as though he might die or that if he didn't, he would need all kinds of care he hadn't needed before. I could see my aunt's misery, and I began to be afraid I would end up in a foster home, something that terrified me. The day it all happened, it was raining. I came home from school, expecting to find the house empty. Aunt Meg was sitting in the kitchen, crying.

"You know how much I love you, Chris," she said, and it was as though she'd said the reverse. I just knew I was going to be cast out. "Gene is very sick, honey. Uncle Will is over there now. How would you like to go to St. Stephen's for a while, till Gene is better?"

I was so happy not to be sent away to live with foster parents that I almost laughed. "But I'm not eighteen. They won't take me."

"I've talked to them, darling. They understand the problem we have with Gene, and they know you want to enter. They said it would be all right."

We went upstairs and packed all my clothes, summer and winter. By the time we were finished, it was time for dinner. We sat and ate, Aunt Meg reassuring me over and over until I realized it was herself she was reassuring. When dinner was done, we took the bags out to the car in the rain.

To my surprise, I found that there were grocery bags full of things that Aunt Meg had bought earlier in the day, soap and a toothbrush and toothpaste, toilet paper and napkins for my periods. There was a generous month's supply of all the toiletries I would need. The rest of what I needed for the first year would come out of my dowry, a requirement of the convent.

I don't know how she got us there. The weather got only worse, and between the rain on the windshield and the tears she kept wiping away, I really believed that some divine intervention guided us. It was the darkest night of my life. Even parked near the Mother House, you could hardly see the lights inside.

The door was opened by a rather tall nun who introduced herself as Sister Joseph. I will probably never meet anyone as compassionate and intelligent as she. She had been assigned as my spiritual director; as I grew older, she became my friend. I know that I was so frightened that night that it would be hard to imagine that anything in my life could frighten me more. I had lost my mother, and now I was losing my aunt and uncle. I had romanticized St. Stephen's and longed for the day when I could enter the convent, but now that I was there, years younger than the youngest novice, I wanted to be anywhere else on earth. Somehow Joseph understood.

I could see that Aunt Meg didn't want to leave. She must have been going through an awful turmoil, doubting her decision, wondering whether she couldn't somehow have managed to keep us all together. Joseph gave her coffee, left us alone for a few minutes, and finally encouraged her to leave. I can't even think of that night without crying.

The miracle is that it worked. In a way, I became everybody's darling and I grew to love them back and to love St. Stephen's. Eventually I took the name Edward Frances, after my father and mother. Aunt Meg, God bless her, never abandoned me. She visited, and her home was the only place I visited for many years. The nuns sent me to a Catholic high school in the next town, and then, when I was seventeen, I entered St. Stephen's College. When I graduated with honors and said I wanted to teach, they sent me off to get my master's at a college where I had my own little apartment and learned the little I know of cooking.

It was a wonderful life for many years, the best life I could have had. The change came when I was in my late twenties. I found that what I loved was the teaching, the students, the reading, not being a nun who did all those things. I watched students graduate and go on, and I knew I wanted to be one of them. I wanted to move on. I found that what I loved in the church was the ritual, all that I had grown up with, that I was comfortable with. I will never be anything but a Catholic, but my faith was no longer the center of my life.

I struggled with all this, wanting to remain faithful to my vows. Eventually I talked to Joseph, and together, we worked it out. When I was absolutely certain, I made my application to be released from my vows. Because we were a pontifical community, I had to write to the Pope. It took nearly a year for my release, and I stayed on till the end of the school year. Because of Aunt Meg's illness, I did a lot of traveling back and forth during that year, but I wanted to be at the college to see my last classes through to the end.

After that, I came to Oakwood.

It had grown dark while I was telling Jack my story. The only light came from the kitchen, the same kitchen where Aunt Meg had told me, fifteen years ago, that I was to go to St. Stephen's that night.

"Gene got better, didn't he?" Jack asked, the first thing he'd said since I'd started.

"Much better. When he got out of his teens, he seemed to shake off all those other problems. We watch him, of course, but his health has really been remarkable."

"Did you tell me all this to explain why you're not going to let me take you to bed?"

"Not tonight, no. But that wasn't the reason. I care about you, and I wanted you to know as much about me as I know about you. And that you're the first man in my life, something I didn't expect to happen for a long time, something I didn't really want to happen so soon."

"Things don't always happen the way you plan them."

"I know that better than anyone. But I want you to understand that if I make a misstep in the etiquette of love, it's because I've never been here before.''

He kissed me then and said something very nice. "Maybe I haven't either.''

When he had left, I went up to Aunt Meg's bedroom, the bedroom I had not taken as my own last month because of the mirror. It was time, I thought, now that I had talked about it.

Standing in front of the dresser where I could see myself, I took off all my clothes and looked at my nude reflection. I had not seen my own body or anyone else's in fifteen years. But I knew now that the day would come when someone else would see mine, and I wanted to see it first.

And in looking, I admitted to myself how much I wanted him.

26

I could have done it by telephone, but I felt that a face-to-face meeting would be best. So on Sunday morning I drove to Brooklyn and parked as close as I could to Mrs. Talley's old building on Ocean Avenue.

I rang the bell, heard the query, and responded. The door loosened at the buzz, and I took the elevator up to the fourth floor. The little round lady with the plump cheeks opened the door as I got off the elevator.

"It's nice to have company on Sunday,'' she said, welcoming me.

"You're not expecting anyone today?''

"Not till three. My granddaughter is bringing her newest boyfriend to meet Grandma."

We had sat in our usual places in the living room. "I bet you approve before you even see him."

She gave me a big smile. "You know me already, and we've hardly been introduced."

"Mrs. Franklin, what I'm going to say is hard for me, but I want you to hear it. You're a lovely lady, and I know what you've been living with for the past forty years." I watched her face change, the smile leave, the eyes narrow. "I know what happened that day that Mrs. Talley was killed. I know you were home; I know you heard the terrible noise in the kitchen and you banged your broom on the ceiling to make the noise stop." I looked through the many-paned glass swinging door to her own kitchen. "I know you went upstairs to complain and you rang the doorbell, but no one answered." I didn't know it, but it seemed the likeliest possibility. She herself had told me that her friend who lived next door heard no noise from the Talley apartment. The walls were thick, but sounds of pounding feet and falling objects could be heard through the floor and ceiling below.

The plumpness in her face seemed to wither as she took in what I was saying.

"I'm not blaming you. They made a lot of noise, and they made no effort to stop it. You must have been very angry when you went upstairs, and even angrier when they pretended not to be home, not to have heard you ring." I watched her. Her eyes were no longer on mine but somewhere far away, maybe forty years away. "Or maybe," I went on, "you guessed, when it suddenly got quiet in the apartment after you rang, that something was going on that was different from the usual noise. Maybe you knew someone was in there doing something so terrible that you were better off not knowing what it was." It was a chance, just a small one, but I had to take it, hoping it would pay off.

She shrank deep into her comfortable chair, looking so sad that I felt terrible. Finally she said, "I won't ask you how you know. When it happened, I took a chance that nobody would know I heard and they would leave me alone. I knew something was very bad when I rang the bell and the noise stopped just like that. I knew I should call the police, but then I thought, whoever it is in there, he knows it's the people downstairs at the door, because I banged on the ceiling. If I call and he gets away, what keeps him from coming after me? From hurting my children? I didn't know he killed anyone. You must believe me.''

''I do believe you, Mrs. Franklin. All I want to know is, did you see him?''

''In my whole life I could never believe I would lie to the police. By the time they came to me with their questions, it was Monday, three days later. What did it matter on Monday? Did I want my picture all over the front page of the paper telling everyone I heard a murder and did nothing?''

I knew she wanted forgiveness, and I had already tried to give it to her, but I sensed she needed more. Perhaps forgiveness is what everybody wants in unlimited quantities. ''The press can be very cruel,'' I said. ''I understand how you felt.''

''I kept quiet. My mother, may she rest in peace, always said, 'If you have nothing to say, say nothing.' I never even told my husband.'' This last seemed to affect her more than anything else. She pulled a tissue out of her dress pocket and patted her eyes.

I got up and went over to her chair. She was so tiny, she was almost lost in it. I knelt beside the chair, feeling her thick carpet under my knees, and took her hand. ''All I want to know is whether you saw him, Mrs. Franklin.''

She nodded her head, and I felt that surge of excitement. ''In the hallway, next to the elevator, is the incinerator. On every floor it's the same. I thought, if this man, whoever he is, comes out, I should see who he is. Maybe I know him. Maybe he lives right here in the building. I went to the incinerator room, and I waited. It was maybe twenty minutes, maybe a little more. I heard Mrs. Talley's door open and close and in the crack of the door where I was, I saw somebody coming out and walking down the hall to the elevator.

I opened the incinerator and closed it with a bang, and I went out. My best friend, Harriet Cohen, I told you, lived next door to the Talleys. I could go there if he was still waiting for the elevator, but I didn't have to. He opened the door to the stairs and went down.''

"You saw him."

"Yes, it was a man, a young man in a big black coat that was too big for him, his hair already creeping back from his forehead. He had his hands in his pockets. His face looked angry, but in New York everybody looks angry. I don't pay it any attention.''

"What did you do?"

"I went back to the Talleys and rang the bell. Maybe I heard a sound, maybe I didn't. Nobody answered. I went downstairs. After that it was quiet.''

"Had you ever seen him before?"

She screwed up her face and shrugged. "Maybe I saw him, maybe I didn't. It was a face. That's all.''

"How old do you think he was? Twenty? Thirty?"

"Halfway in between."

"So he could be alive today." I stood and walked to the window.

"God forbid."

"Thank you, Mrs. Franklin. I know how hard this was for you.''

"You're a smart girl to figure all this out."

"I had some help," I told her honestly. "Have a good time with your granddaughter today. Don't get up. I can get out myself.''

But she had pushed herself out of the chair and was following me to the door. "I have to double-lock it," she said. "You can't be too careful.''

I drove directly to Greenwillow. I wanted to check out the twins, make sure they had come through yesterday's ordeal all right. I was in for a shock.

A staff member opened the door, and when I asked for the

twins, she said, "Robert's here, but James is in the hospital."

My heart sank. "What happened?"

"Some kind of a stomach upset. They decided to keep him overnight."

"Let me take Robert to see him."

"I don't think that would be wise," she said.

"It's absolutely necessary." I sounded as authoritarian as I could. "Those twins are lost without each other. Where's Robert?"

"In his room."

I flew up the stairs, found Robert, and took him to the hospital, which adjoined the Greenwillow wing. When the twins saw each other, they locked eyes as they had the evening of the Fourth, and then they relaxed, their lives joined once again.

"How are you, James?" I asked.

"My stomach hurts."

I was going to ask if he'd seen the doctor, but I remembered he couldn't tell me anything if he experienced it alone. "Stay here," I said. "I want to find the doctor."

It was Sunday, so a nurse was all I could find, but she was very helpful.

"The doctor suspects some kind of food poisoning," she said when I had explained who I was. "The lab report should be back tomorrow."

"Was anyone else at Greenwillow affected?"

"Apparently not. It probably wasn't what he had for lunch. He was holding a candy wrapper when he started vomiting."

"I'm leaving the second twin here for a while. I've got to talk to someone at Greenwillow."

She sputtered that she couldn't handle both of them, but I assured her there would be no trouble and I ran. Back at Greenwillow I asked for the source of the candy bars that had been given out the day before.

"We didn't give any out," the cook said.

"James Talley was given a candy bar," I told her. "If he didn't get it from the kitchen, where did it come from?"

"Don't ask me. All I know is it's not on the list." She handed me the previous day's menus. "There was ice cream at three-thirty. No candy bars." She sounded irritated.

"Maybe there was a guest who gave them out. If there was something wrong, they should be told. Other residents might get sick, too."

"Ask Jonesy. She was on duty yesterday." The cook turned away.

Jonesy looked at the log and said two residents had been picked up to spend the day with their families, but no guests stayed for a snack, and no one else complained of stomach trouble.

I was starting to feel very uneasy. "Do you mind if I question the residents?" I asked.

She looked undecided.

"Call Virginia if you need backing up."

That seemed to do it. She clearly didn't want her authority undermined. "Go ahead. I'm sure you'll be appropriately courteous."

Appropriately courteous. I thanked her and left before she had misgivings. I started with Gene, who didn't know what I was talking about. Then I went from resident to resident, slowly, appropriately courteous in demeanor. It took a long time and I listened to a lot of digressions, but I finally hit pay dirt.

A very sweet blond girl who was often in Gene's activity groups admitted she had given James and Robert the candy bars.

"Did a lady give them to you?" I asked, wanting to establish her reliability.

"No."

"Did a man give them to you?"

"Yes."

"What did the man say?"

"Give to those twinmen."

"And you gave the candy bars to the twinmen?"

"Yes."

"Did the man give you a candy bar?"

"Yes."

"Did you eat it?"

"Yes."

"Was it good?"

"Yes." She smiled. "I like candy bars."

"So do I. Did you know the man, Jenny?"

"Uh-uh."

"Where did you see him?"

She stuck out her arm and pointed toward the delivery area, where trucks sometimes drove in to drop off food.

I thanked her and sent her off to her friends. Then I returned to the hospital.

I spent some time with the twins, finally getting a resident to agree to release James to Greenwillow. It seemed safe enough; he couldn't be closer to a hospital if he needed one, and I felt it was more important that the twins be together than that James have a nurse nearby.

From Greenwillow I called Virginia and told her what had happened and what I had learned. She knew of James's stomach upset but didn't know the cause. She assured me she would keep the twins indoors until we found out what was going on.

I went home and called Jack, but there was no answer. I felt restless, but nothing seemed to satisfy me, not reading, not TV. On a whim, I took myself to the closest town with a movie theater and sat for two hours watching a film. It helped to calm me down. On the way home, I stopped at a pizzeria and bought a very sloppy sandwich of sausage and green peppers, which I ate at home. I called Jack again, but he was still out.

I wondered whether Melanie was home, and looked her number up. In small towns like Oakwood, one of the service organizations usually provides an annual telephone directory, twenty or thirty pages in large, readable type. Running my finger down the page looking for Gross, I stopped at Gore. Betsy Gore had stopped me at the beach yesterday afternoon. I noted that her husband's name was Daniel.

I stopped and tried to recall the name of the man who had

called Friday evening to inquire about my progress. My mind
was a blank. I rummaged on the counter next to the phone.
I often take notes on the backs of envelopes and then hesitate
to throw them away, in case I need the information later. It's
not very efficient or tidy, but I never seem to have a notepad
when I need one.

The Friday envelope was still there. Harry Forrest on Sunset Drive. I flipped back two pages from Gore and looked
through the Fs. No Forrest, no Forest. No Forster or Foster.
I started feeling a little sick.

In the centerfold of the stapled directory was a pen-and-
ink map of Oakwood with the names of all the streets listed
alphabetically along the sides of the pages. There was no
Sunset, no Sunrise, no Sunshine, no Sun.

My heart was now beating in a panicky nonrhythm. I
picked up the phone and dialed information.

"The number of Harry Forrest in Oakwood," I said.

There was the kind of pause that told me she hadn't found
it on her first search.

"I don't find a listing for Harry Forrest in Oakwood."

"Maybe they have an unlisted number," I suggested.

"I'm sorry, there is no Forrest in Oakwood."

"Thank you."

I put the phone down and leaned against the doorjamb.
The man who had called had known my name and my phone
number. It was a cinch he knew my address. The day after
he had called, one of the twins had come down with a "stomach upset" that had hospitalized him. Both of the twins had
been given candy bars from a mysterious man, *but only one
twin had gotten sick.* Was it possible that Jerry was alive and
well and protecting his interests?

27

I called Jack at eight on Monday morning and told him everything. Although he sounded perfectly calm, his reaction was like overkill. He wanted me to come to Brooklyn and stay at his apartment. I refused adamantly.

"This isn't sex, Chris. It's protection."

"I didn't think it was sex." Well, maybe I did. "I want to stay near the twins. They've grown fond of me and they trust me."

"Damn it, this guy's a killer."

"Well, it won't do him any good to kill me. If anyone's in danger, it's the twins."

"Why do you expect a killer to act rationally?"

"Jack, I'm not leaving here. I'm going to call my neighbors and ask them to keep an eye on my house. If they see anyone around, or a strange car, they can call the police."

"Terrific." I could hear the sarcasm in his voice. "I'll come to see you and get shot in the back by a trigger-happy neighbor with a hunting rifle or some country cop on his first stakeout."

"I'll get a special dispensation for you," I said softly.

"Chris, I'm not kidding."

"Neither am I. I'll keep in touch. I have some calls to make today, and I want to check with the hospital on the lab report."

He wasn't happy, but I remained firm and we left it that way. I did as I promised and spoke to my neighbors, all of whom assured me they would stay alert. A little after nine, I made my first long-distance call.

It was to New Hope, the institution where James had spent forty dismal years of what some people called life. I asked the operator who answered how she handled calls about patient information.

"I got a number I send them to," she said.

"Could you give me that number?"

"Sure."

A woman answered. I told her I was trying to find someone related to James Talley, who had been released several months ago, and I wondered whether anyone had ever called for information on him.

"His cousin did," she answered with no hesitation.

"His cousin?"

"He always said, 'This is James's cousin Joe. How's he doing?' "

"How often did he call?"

"About once a month. Before Christmas. That kind of thing."

"So he knew when James was transferred to Greenwillow."

"I told him myself."

I made a similar call to Robert's institution and got similar answers. Then I called the residence in Buffalo.

"Yes, I think someone did call a couple of times," the woman who answered told me.

"His cousin?"

"It may have been a cousin."

"Do you recall when he called for the last time?"

"I do. It was just before the Fourth. I told him Robert was moving to Greenwillow and it might be permanent."

"Thank you."

I didn't really have to call Greenwillow, but I did, just to satisfy myself that the chain had been completed. "Cousin Joe" had been calling Greenwillow to check upon James since about a week after his arrival. And last Thursday, July fifth, he had called to see how both his "cousins" were doing.

"I told him you were the driving force behind getting the twins together," she said. "He seemed really pleased."

I'll bet, I thought. "Thank you," I said.

After I hung up, Virginia called. "I've got some very frightening news," she said. "I've just seen the lab report. Someone injected a very powerful poison into that candy bar. That was no Halloween prank. I think someone wanted James dead."

"Somebody did," I said. I remembered what one of the twins had said when we were taping on Saturday. Jerry was nice. Jerry had brought them chocolate.

Jerry was ready to kill—again.

I had nowhere else to turn, so I went back to the papers Dr. Sanderson had sent. Over the next couple of hours I read the ones I had not yet looked at. James and Robert were described in each of these papers, sometimes quite cavalierly—"a pair of savant twins with the mental capacities of five-year olds"—and the results of "games" were detailed. There was very little that was new to me, but I found that the papers with the most names listed as authors lacked Dr. Weintraub's easy, thoughtful style. I suspected the "junior collaborators" in those articles were the soldiers who had done much of the compiling of the data and the actual writing, younger people on their way up, among whom might be the elusive Jerry, although none of the names seemed probable.

Only one article looked promising, a paper by Henry Courtland, M.D., in which he discussed the length of time it took the twins to come up with answers (like prime numbers, dates, or days of the week), clocked with a stopwatch, and described how they looked at each other during the process. I wondered if Dr. Courtland might have been on to something. Also, although the papers were heavily footnoted, most of the references were to older works of the same kind, some of them dating to the nineteenth century. But Dr. Courtland, at the point of discussing the twins' looking into each other's eyes, wrote in a footnote, "See also my paper in *Psychological Review*," followed by the date and volume number.

I called around Westchester until I found a library with a complete set of *Psychological Review*. Then I cut myself a piece of Swiss cheese, drank a glass of juice, folded the article into my bag, and drove off.

The journal was bound, and I found the Courtland article with little difficulty. It was clear he thought the twins' habit of looking at each other intently as they came up with answers to questions was important to the process, but his opinion was that they were giving each other moral support. He spent most of the article talking about other retarded people who displayed remarkable gifts. But in the sentence where the twins were mentioned, there was a footnote: "See also 'The Role of Visual Contact in the Performance of Savant Twins,' G. K. Spanner, Dept. of Psychology, unpublished papers."

My heart nearly stopped. Maybe we had a Gerry instead of a Jerry! I hurried home and called the NYU School of Medicine. They had an address for Dr. Henry Courtland, who had retired a few years ago to Florida, and I persuaded the young woman to give me the phone number. Two minutes later I was on the phone with Dr. Courtland.

I went through my explanation and refreshed his memory. He recalled the twins well, although he had not seen them very often. He had accompanied Dr. Weintraub on a few occasions, but their interests were different. Dr. Courtland was involved at that time in studying how people recalled facts and solved problems in their heads. When Dr. Weintraub told him that the twins seemed to take increasingly longer to generate increasingly larger prime numbers, Dr. Courtland thought it was worth some investigation.

"I've just read your article in *Psychological Review*," I told him. "You've got a footnote there that intrigues me. Something about an unpublished paper, 'The Role of Visual Contact in the Performance of Savant Twins,' by G. K. Spanner."

"Oh, Gerry Spanner. I haven't thought of him for years."

"What can you tell me about him, Dr. Courtland?"

"Well, if you want a very unscientific opinion, I thought he was nuts." He laughed at his own joke.

I chuckled to show my appreciation. "In what way?"

"As a person, he had a nasty temper. The slightest thing could set him off, so it was tough going working with him. And professionally, Gerry thought there was some kind of ESP going on between the Talley twins, that they couldn't perform unless they were in the same room, or something like that. Frankly, I always put ESP in a class with witchcraft, but he was very adamant."

"Was he a medical student?"

"Good heavens, no. He was in the psych department, but he knew someone, maybe one of Dr. Weintraub's associates, and got to see the twins that way."

"Did he publish those findings?"

"I wouldn't call them 'findings.' They were guesses at best. And he couldn't publish. He wanted to use the idea as the basis for his doctoral dissertation. You can't use previously published material for that, as I'm sure you know."

I did know, having done a master's essay some years ago. "What was this 'unpublished paper' you referred to in your article?"

"It was a talk he gave to the psychology club or some such thing. When he heard about my study, he asked me to footnote his 'paper,' if that's what you would call it. He thought it would enhance his small reputation. I agreed, frankly because I wanted to get rid of him. He was making a pest of himself."

"Dr. Courtland, do you know of any plans he had to take the twins away from their mother for the purpose of his study?"

"Oh, he had some grandiose idea. He wanted to put them in a controlled environment and study them together and separately. He wanted to see whether they responded with a wall between them, with their backs to each other, at various distances. If he'd been able to prove anything, it would have been an excellent dissertation topic."

The "hiding game," I thought, realizing I had jumped to a wrong conclusion that they had played hide-and-seek. "He didn't do it, though, did he?"

"No, and no one seems to know what happened to him. I think he dropped out after the killing. I suppose having the twins in jail spoiled his plans. As I recall, they were sent to separate institutions."

"They were. So he never got his Ph.D."

"Not that I know of, but I really had nothing to do with the psych department. You could call over there; I'm sure they'd tell you. But I'm pretty certain someone told me he'd given up altogether, went into the family business or some such thing."

"Do you recall his first name, Doctor?"

"Gerard, I think it was."

I thanked him very much and hung up. Then I tried Jack, but he wasn't at the precinct. I pulled out Aunt Meg's worn old copy of the Manhattan directory and looked up Spanner. There was no G., G. K., or Gerard. I called Information, and they confirmed that there was no listing. The same was true in Westchester. It occurred to me that he might live anywhere in the country. The calls to New Hope and Greenwillow and the other places could have originated anywhere. And if he wasn't living in the area, but had come in to do harm to the twins, there was no telling where he was staying now, if anywhere. He might be holing up in a station wagon or van.

It was now late afternoon, and my chances of getting any more information from the university or the medical school were slim. I went out to the car and drove to Greenwillow.

The twins were in their room replaying a scene from the 1940s, which, after all, was practically yesterday in their memory. I stood at the door watching them until James turned and saw me.

"Look, it's Chris," he said happily.

I went in and talked to them for a while. James was feeling much better. Remnants of tea and bouillon on a tray told me what he'd been eating, and his cheerful demeanor told me much more.

I stayed an hour, then went home and tried Jack. He was still out somewhere, or maybe, I thought, he'd gone home for the day. But he wasn't at that number either.

Although there were still a couple of hours of daylight left, I went around the first floor and closed blinds, shades, and curtains. Feeling rather foolish, I went down to the basement and looked around. Aunt Meg's supply of canned goods was arranged on shelves built into the wall, and a pile of my cartons, still unopened, stood nearby. The patio furniture was piled in a corner. There was a furnace and a water heater, which turned on while I was there, nearly sending me into a panic. Otherwise, the basement was fairly empty.

Four small, hinged windows, two on the front and two on the back of the house, all seemed to be closed and latched. I wasn't very hungry, but I went upstairs, made a salad, and ate it while reading the paper.

When I was finished, I sat at the dining room table and made a list of all the coauthors of all the articles Dr. Sanderson had sent me. Most of the names were repeated from article to article, so the final list was less than ten. Tomorrow I would try to locate each of them and see if anyone remembered or, better still, had kept in touch with Gerard Spanner.

That done, I found the book I was reading and got myself comfortable on the sofa. I would have liked to play some music or even watch television, but Jack had made me so nervous that I thought I ought to keep it quiet so that I could hear if a car approached or someone tried to break in.

As it turned out, I didn't hear anything until the doorbell rang, and when it did, I froze. Suddenly I felt very alone and very vulnerable. I got up and walked nearer the front door, being careful not to stand in front of it.

"Who is it?" Hoping I didn't sound terrified.

"Jack."

I felt as though I'd had a reprieve from the gallows. I opened the door and he came in and held me. I heard the door close and realized he must have kicked it shut. Then we kissed.

"You okay?"

"Fine."

"How about putting some clothes in a bag and coming home with me, just for overnight?"

I considered it. "We'd have to go in two cars. I can't spend tomorrow in New York."

He said, "Shit," under his breath. Then, "Chris, I don't think you're safe here."

The phone rang, startling me. I went to get it.

"Chris?" a woman's voice said.

"Yes."

"Are you all right?"

"I'm fine. Who's this?"

"Midge McGuire next door. I was taking the dog for a walk and I saw a car in your driveway. You said to look out—"

"Oh, thanks, Midge. A friend just dropped by. I really appreciate it."

"I hope you don't mind—"

"Mind? I think you're wonderful."

She assured me she'd keep her watch, and we said good-bye.

The phone call seemed to change Jack's mind a little about my leaving, and anyway, I was determined not to go.

"Okay," he said, finally, "I'll stay till morning."

"Let me make up the guest room."

"I'm staying down here."

"You'll be more comfortable—"

"I'll do more good down here."

We talked for a while and then I got him a towel and a pillow. While I was fixing up the sofa, he pulled a gun out of a holster around his ankle and put it on the end table. I must have looked surprised.

"No jacket in summer," he explained. "Nowhere else to carry it."

"Must make it tough to swim," I said.

"Makes a lot of things tough." He gave me a kiss. "Go to sleep and don't worry about anything."

I didn't sleep well. I heard things, I imagined things. I wondered if Jack was comfortable.

At about three in the morning I put my robe on and tiptoed down the stairs. I hadn't even gotten to the last step when I heard his voice from the dark living room.

"Go back to sleep. Everything's fine."

I said, "Good night," and went back upstairs. After that I slept.

28

I spent most of the next day making fruitless phone calls. The Psychology Department at NYU thought I was crazy to be looking for someone from forty years ago. The secretary said she might be able to help me, but it would take time. Records that old were stored away, and she couldn't get to them today. The registrar found Gerard K. Spanner but said that he hadn't registered since the 1950 spring term. His last known address was Newark, New Jersey, but it was unlikely he was still there. Newark, they assured me, had changed. The alumni office had no address and asked me to give them one if I found him. Sure thing.

Then I got the status and whereabouts of the coauthors of the papers Dr. Sanderson had sent me. Two were dead, three were in New York, one in Los Angeles, one outside of Chicago, and one in Boston. I started on the East Coast and worked my way west. It was a thankless task. Most of the doctors were seeing patients or unavailable. I managed to talk to two. Both remembered the Talley twins; neither had ever heard of Gerry Spanner. I got the feeling from one of them that his circle of friends didn't include psychologists.

Jack had said he would try to find Spanner through Motor Vehicles, but I didn't hear from him, so I assumed he'd failed to turn up the name. I called and left a message saying Spanner had lived in Newark in 1950 and could he try New Jersey Motor Vehicles, too?

Finally I got in my car and drove to Greenwillow.

The twins were fine, Gene was fine, Virginia McAlpin was fine. The doctor had been to see James, who was recovering nicely. No one had called about the twins or tried to see them except me. I hung around for a while and then, satisfied that they were safe, went home.

One of my neighbors waved as I came down Pine Brook Road, and I stopped and chatted, reminding her to stay alert. A car came along, and I left her and pulled into the driveway. Since I didn't plan to go out again tonight, I put the car in the garage and shut the door.

The garbage had been collected, and the tops to the cans were askew. I straightened them up and went into the house.

Life is composed of a lot of patterns. The one I follow when I enter the house is to go to the kitchen and drop my bag and keys on the counter. After that, I think about what I want to do.

So on that afternoon I followed my usual pattern, went to the kitchen, dropped my bag on the counter and my keys next to it, and turned to the refrigerator to get some juice. What I saw as I turned was a glistening on the floor, as though someone had spilled water. It puzzled me, because there was no water around and the ceiling was quite dry. I walked toward it—it was near the window that faced the backyard—and realized it wasn't water; it was shattered glass. *A pane of the window had been broken!*

It took a moment to register. Someone had broken a pane of my kitchen window. *Someone was in this house!* I swiveled on my sandal, making a dash for the telephone. Aunt Meg had taped the emergency number on the side of the phone, and I knew the Oakwood police were very responsive. I picked up the receiver and put it to my ear. There was no dial tone, and looking down, I could see that someone had removed the thin wire connecting the base of the telephone with the little box on the wall.

I needed nothing else to tell me to get out of the house, and fast. I grabbed my bag and keys and started for the door. I didn't get there.

He must have been hiding in the closet near the stairs, because suddenly he was in front of me, a man in his sixties who could have been my father except that he was holding a gun. I stopped dead.

"So that's what you look like," he said, his eyes appraising me.

"What do you want?"

"You know what I want."

"I don't." I really didn't. What I was trying to decide was whether to let him know how much I knew or play dumb. If I knew nothing, would he have any reason to kill me?

He solved my dilemma. "You keep nice careful notes, Miss B. I like a well-organized woman."

The dining room table! Practically everything I knew was written down in the order in which I had learned it. "There's more," I said. "Things that aren't on the table."

"Sure."

"There are tapes."

"Of what?"

"Of the twins' recollections of Good Friday. They've been turned over to the New York City police."

"Sure," he said again.

"It's true."

"It doesn't matter. They're worthless in a court of law."

I had no idea whether that was true or not, but a tape could certainly be forged quite easily. "And the police know your name. I got it from Dr. Henry Courtland."

"That old bastard still alive?"

"Quite alive. And he remembers you well."

"If he'd given me the slightest chance, I could have done

what I wanted. What I discovered was the biggest break-through in the study of the mind in this century.''

"I know that. I admire you for your discovery."

"I don't need your admiration, Miss B. I need your help."

"I can't help you."

"You don't have a choice." He wagged the gun.

"Mr. Spanner, I'm sure you killed Mrs. Talley by acci-dent." I knew from the twins that wasn't true, but I wanted to keep him calm. Dr. Courtland had said he had a nasty temper, and the twins' story of the murder reinforced that.

He stared at me coldly for several seconds. "Don't sweet-talk me, lady. I killed someone who got in my way. That's the long and short of it.''

It wasn't the long and short of it as far as I was concerned. Forgetting my resolve to keep from angering him, I said, "You also condemned two innocent men to forty years in prison."

"They didn't know the difference. And if I couldn't have them, I wanted to make damn sure no one could."

"It was a long time ago. They would never try you now. Why don't you confess and get it off your conscience?'' I knew it was a foolishly Catholic thing to say to a man who had probably abandoned his code of morals decades ago, if he'd ever had one.

"My idea is much easier and much quicker. You and I go to Greenwillow, and you get me one of the twins. I don't care which one. It's your choice. You give him to me, and I go back to the identity I've been using for the last forty years. You see, it doesn't make much difference whether you know my name or not. Gerry Spanner's been dead and buried for a long time. Let's go." He waved the gun toward the side door.

I stared at him without moving. I was to choose a twin for him to kill! Echoes of World War II reverberated in my head. This man wanted me to select who would live and who would die. He would make me his accomplice. And then what? Then he would kill me.

A hundred things went through my mind. If we stayed

here long enough, Jack would probably show up and even the odds. He might be calling me now for all I knew. With the phones disconnected, it would probably just sound like a ring to him and he would assume I had gone out. But it seemed that my best bet was to stay in the house as long as possible.

"I can't get the twins for you during daylight," I said, trying to sound calm. "Since you tried to poison James on Saturday, they've been held indoors."

"I don't intend to get them during daylight. I want to get you out of this house before your boyfriend arrives to spend the night."

He had been watching the house. I felt my options decreasing. If only I could leave a message for Jack; if only I could . . . It was hopeless. I turned toward the front door, a small, tenuous idea starting to percolate.

"Not that way," Spanner said. "Back door."

It wasn't much, but I managed to walk outside leaving the back door unlocked. If Jack tried it—and why would he?— he would think it odd. But he might come in and see the broken window. It was a chance.

"We're taking your car."

I started down the driveway, wishing I could see a neighbor. But like the legendary elusive policeman, there weren't any around when I needed them.

I backed out of the drive, leaving the garage door open, something I ordinarily took care not to do, but who would know that? I wished there were some small thing I could drop—a wallet, a pen—but my bag was now on the floor of the car next to Spanner's feet, and I had nothing available to toss.

"I know the way, so don't do anything stupid. Drive carefully. When we get there, I'll tell you where to park."

To get to Greenwillow, you pass through several little towns, each with its own school system, police force, and volunteer fire fighters. There were cars on the road, and we even passed a police car, which I looked at longingly, but I was afraid to flick on the emergency flasher; Spanner would not miss that.

Finally I started seeing signs to the hospital, and I put my signal on.

"Drive right by the hospital and keep going."

"Where are we going?"

"You'll see when we get there."

Where we were going was the local hamburger place. Gerry Spanner was hungry and obviously thought he had a long night ahead of him. He should have been a cop, I thought, nearly smiling.

We ordered food at the drive-through window and sat in the parking lot eating. I wasn't very hungry, but I managed to drink something. Spanner ate as though he hadn't eaten all day. I toyed with the idea of opening the car door and running, but he had that gun, and even while he ate, he kept it in his hand. I didn't think I'd get very far.

When we finished, he put the waste paper on the backseat and told me to drive to the hospital. We parked some distance away and walked. The hospital and the Greenwillow wing backed up on a section of woods beyond which was a fairly new development of attractive houses. I remember Aunt Meg telling me that the woods belonged to the town, so the home-owners could be sure of having privacy in perpetuity. It also gave Spanner and me a place to sit unseen and be fairly cool in the warm evening.

It was a long wait. Most of the residents came outside after dinner, but I could see the lights on in the lounge, where several probably sat watching TV.

"How do you plan to get inside?" I asked when we had been sitting for quite some time. "The doors are all kept locked."

"Let me worry about that."

"I don't see what you need me for."

That was what puzzled me. He didn't answer, and I kept thinking about it. He had used a Greenwillow resident to get the candy to the twins on Saturday, but he couldn't try that again. The twins were being kept indoors, and he had to be able to monitor the messenger. (He couldn't chance giving a poisoned candy bar to a resident who would disappear inside the building, possibly to eat it himself.)

And he couldn't trust me to go inside and come out with one of the twins. I wouldn't do it. I would call the police from the nearest phone.

So if he knew how to get in, what did he need me for? It's funny about puzzles. When you see the answer, you can't imagine why you didn't see it before.

Gerry Spanner didn't know which room the twins lived in. He needed me to show him. He couldn't go from room to room without waking a number of residents and causing a stir. Once I saw that, I knew exactly what I had to do. It was chancy and might put an innocent person in jeopardy, but I had no other choice.

We watched the residents go inside at dusk. One by one, lights went on in the bedrooms. Another hour passed. I wanted desperately to stand, stretch, run in place, but every time my movements made a crunch, Spanner turned on me with a glare that said everything.

I tried several times to engage Spanner in conversation. I had grandiose ideas of distracting him, disarming him, dissuading him. Although I knew the chances of doing any of those things were very slim, I had to try. But Spanner had no interest in conversation. He sat slightly behind me and to my left so that he could see my every move, and whenever I tried to talk, he shushed me brusquely.

The lights started to go out. The sky was now dark and I could no longer read my watch, but if Jack had driven up from New York, he would have arrived hours ago. I had kept my eyes peeled, but had seen him nowhere.

I wasn't sure how many staff members slept at Greenwillow, but two lights remained stubbornly lit after all the others were out. I could imagine someone lying in bed with a good book—how I wished I were in my own!—until the wee hours. I was so tired that I fell asleep against a tree, waking with a start when Spanner nudged me.

"Get up," he ordered.

I had to orient myself for a minute. Then I stood, found my bag on the ground, and followed him toward the building.

He kept one hand wrapped tightly around my upper arm, tugging at it to stop me, to move forward, to slow me down. He knew where we were going, so I assumed he had scouted the area sometime earlier.

We came out behind the hospital and moved toward the Greenwillow wing, staying close to the building. We actually entered the hospital itself through a door that led to the basement level. There was a laundry on one side of the hall, and some doors fitted with wired glass panes behind which there was no light. I don't like hospitals, probably because almost everyone I've ever visited in them died. Although we were far from any patients, it was eerie and the hall was dimly lighted, and my distaste was palpable.

Spanner led the way to a door which opened into a dark area.

"This way," he said.

We came to a flight of stairs, at the top of which was another door, and that one opened into the Greenwillow kitchen. In the moonlight I could see pots hanging from hooks, the large refrigerator, the huge institutional stove. Spanner's fingers were pressing into my flesh, hurting me and angering me.

We came out of the kitchen and walked into the entrance area. It was dark and empty.

"You know where their room is?" he asked in a whisper.

"Yes."

"Let's go."

We went up the stairs and down the hall. I walked purposely past the Talleys' room and stopped at my cousin Gene's.

"This it?"

"Yes." I wondered if he could tell I was shaking.

"I'll be out here. Get me one of the twins." He moved back down the hall toward the stairs.

I went inside and woke Gene. "Gene," I said softly, "it's me, Kix."

"Kix?"

"Yes. Listen, do you know where Jonesy's room is?"

He nodded.

"Can you count to twenty?"

"Yes. One, two, three—"

"Shh. That's good. Listen, after I go out, you count to twenty. Then go to Jonesy's room and tell her Chris said to call the police. Can you say that?"

"Kix said call police."

It would have to do. "Okay. That's good. Now, you wait till I'm outside, then count to twenty. Then find Jonesy."

"Okay."

I left him, hoping fervently it would work.

Spanner moved toward me quickly as I left the bedroom. "Where the hell is he?" he said in a whisper.

"I don't know. They changed the room. Somebody else is in there. It's not the twins." I was speaking quietly but out loud. I started down the hall, away from the Talleys' room, away from the stairs. When I got to the next door, I opened it and looked in. "They're not here." I moved forward.

Spanner caught my arm. "Keep your goddamn voice down! You know damn well where they are. Take me to their room." He was in a fury, his voice shaking as it rose in pitch.

"There are some bigger rooms back here," I said, pulling him toward the back of the building. "Let me look." I opened another door and peered in, waiting until I heard Gene open his door behind us and run out. "They're not here." The occupant of the room turned over in bed at the sound of my voice.

Spanner shook me. He was in such a rage, I was afraid he might shoot me just to sate his anger. I had to keep him at bay until the police arrived, which might be five minutes or more.

"You bitch," he said, nearly frothing at the mouth. He pushed me toward the next door, opened it himself, and looked in. A woman sat up in bed, looked at him, and screamed. He slammed the door and went to the next door, which was around a corner.

There were stirrings now in the rooms, but no sound of sirens. What if Gene hadn't delivered the message correctly? What if Jonesy decided to investigate herself, coming upstairs in a nightgown to look around? Spanner would have two hostages instead of one, and a possible panic among the residents.

Suddenly the light went on in the hallway. Spanner pulled me in front of him, pinning my hands in front of me with his arm. In his other hand I could see the gun.

"Spanner," a familiar voice called, "this is Sergeant Brooks of the New York City police. Put your weapon down and walk toward the stairs."

"Jack," I called to let him know I was there. Then I relaxed.

In some ways I am ridiculously naive. When I heard Jack's voice, I really thought it was all over, that Spanner would let me go, put down his gun, and give himself up. I guess that tells you more about me than about anything else. Spanner clearly had no intention of giving up without a fight, and I was to be his shield and his weapon.

We had turned the corner before we heard Jack's voice, and down the hall on the wall was a large EXIT sign lighted in red. I had been present at least once during a fire drill, and the residents knew what "exit" meant and knew how to get out. So, apparently, did Gerry Spanner.

He pushed me toward the fire stairs as I heard someone running toward us from behind. Inside the door there were stairs in both directions. For a moment I thought he was going to try for the roof, but he changed his mind and we started down. He was pushing me so hard, I was afraid I'd fall and kill us both, but somehow I made it to the first floor safely.

As we ran, the door on the second floor opened and a man's voice called, "Let her go, Spanner. There's nowhere you can go now." Footsteps started down the stairs behind us. The voice wasn't Jack's, and I realized the local police had arrived.

"I'll kill her," Spanner shouted, and I thought, He means it. He's desperate.

The gun was along my waist, pointing forward. With a flick of his wrist, Spanner could easily have turned it in to my body.

At the bottom of the stairs, a door opened onto the terrace at the back of the Greenwillow wing. Spanner pushed it open. Lights had been turned on everywhere, and we practically walked into Jack's arms.

"It's okay, Chris," he said, and I nodded.

"Out of the way," Spanner said, and Jack backed off slowly.

Like a snapshot frozen forever, his face at that moment is imprinted in my mind. All the features were the same, but the composite was someone I had never met. There was no almost smile on his lips, no warmth in his eyes, no hint of the low-key, easygoing man I was half in love with.

Spanner turned around and pulled me backward so that we faced Jack, so that if he shot, I would be hit. I couldn't imagine where Spanner was going to take me. My car was parked half a mile away, and I had no idea where his was, if he had one.

Suddenly Jack yelled, "No!" to someone behind us, and Spanner pulled me backward roughly as he leaned against the wall. Two policemen stood facing us to the left while Jack was to our right. I was sure I heard a click as one of the local policemen cocked his gun.

"Drop the guns, cops," Spanner shouted.

Nothing happened. It was like a film frozen on one terrifying frame.

"Now!" Spanner screamed, tightening his hold on me. "I'll kill her. Drop them." He waved his gun around, then brought it back and pushed it into my side.

The three men moved in a kind of crazy slow motion, laying their guns on the ground, then straightening up. Pushing me ahead of him, Spanner picked up all three and dropped them into his shirt. From the look of them, they must have weighed about ten pounds. I could feel them against my back as he pressed me toward him.

"Back," he ordered the two local policemen, and they retreated very slowly to where Jack was standing. Then he pushed me and we started running.

I knew we were heading for the door to the hospital basement. I knew, too, that no one would chance shooting, because a bullet that hit Spanner might go right through him and into me. That had been why Jack had shouted No. We made it through the door, and Spanner took a moment to lock it. Then we started down the long, dim corridor away from Greenwillow.

"Just keep quiet and you may survive this," Spanner said as we ran.

He obviously knew his way around. We passed one stairway and then ducked into another and went up. There was a big "1" on the wall at the head of the stairs, and he pushed the door open. We were on a corridor that stretched endlessly in both directions. Spanner pushed me to the right and we started running again.

By now he was panting hard, his breath hot around my neck. It occurred to me he must be at least in his mid-sixties and he wasn't in especially good shape, or so it seemed to me. I probably had a couple of miles of running ahead of me until I began to feel fatigued, but I was awfully tired. Listening to his labored breathing, smelling the stench of his sweat, I wondered how much longer he could hold out.

It wasn't much. We left the hospital through a fire door on the front side, and Spanner stopped and leaned against the building to catch his breath. In the parking circle near the main entrance to our right I could see a police car with its light rotating on the roof. That was probably Spanner's means of escape. I didn't want it to be my death conveyance. If I got into that car, I was dead. There was no time to think, to figure, to weigh, to measure. It was act now or die. I made my move.

Rallying what was left of my strength, I pulled away from him, heard him shout, "Hey!" and come after me. He grabbed the back of my blouse, and I lost my footing and came down on him.

That was when I heard the explosion. It was so loud and so close that I screamed and pulled away. Spanner had released me. I looked back at him from where I was sitting on the concrete walk. He had keeled over on the ground, and it went through my mind that he must have had a heart attack from the exertion.

Police came charging toward us, some from the left, where Greenwillow was, some from the right, where the entrance to the hospital was. Two armed cops moved in first, their guns pointed at the unmoving Spanner.

Jack was suddenly next to me, shielding my view of Spanner.

"What happened?" I asked.

One of the cops I couldn't see answered my question. "Looks like his arsenal got him."

I felt foggy. "I don't understand."

Jack looked away, then slid his arm around me and held me, both of us sitting on the ground like a couple of children. "One of the guns in his shirt went off."

"Oh no," I said, and I was instantly overcome with the worst case of chills I have ever experienced.

Someone found a blanket for me—we were, after all, outside a hospital—and Spanner was put on a stretcher, the guns removed from his shirt after it was ripped open so that a doctor and nurse could begin working on the wound.

I started thinking again. "Jack, my keys. Spanner put them in his pocket."

Jack wrapped the blanket around me so it would stay in place and got up. There was a conference around the stretcher, and he came back with my keys. My bag was probably somewhere at Greenwillow, most likely on the fire stairs.

At the thought of Greenwillow, my responsibilities came back to me. "I've got to get to Greenwillow," I told him.

"There's time."

"No. Right now."

He talked briefly with a uniformed officer whom I took to

be the local chief of police, and then he came back and helped me up. We were driven the short distance to Greenwillow in a police car. Jonesy opened the front door for us. She looked scared to death.

"Where's my cousin?" I asked as we walked in. "Where's Gene?"

"In my room."

We followed her to her small apartment on the first floor. Gene was sitting on her bed in his pajamas, looking desolate.

"Gene," I said, "are you okay?"

He shook his head.

"What's the matter?"

"No eighteen."

"I don't understand." I sat beside him and put my arm around him.

"No eighteen," he said, and he sounded near tears.

"Did you ask him to count or something?" Jonesy asked.

"Yes. To twenty and then find you."

"Well, he forgot eighteen, and I thought that's what he was coming down and waking me up to ask me."

"Gene," I said, hugging him, "you were wonderful. You were marvelous."

He brightened up. "One, two, three—"

"It doesn't matter. Eighteen doesn't matter. You were a real hero."

He was all smiles.

"Come," I said, "let's get you up to bed."

It turned out the Talley twins had slept through the commotion, so that the events of the night would not be part of their repertoire. Jack took me home, and sitting at the kitchen table with a mug of hot tea, he filled me in on what I didn't already know.

"I started worrying when you didn't answer your phone all afternoon. I called the Oakwood police and asked them to check out your house. They found the broken window, the open door, and the phone cords missing. I got there as fast as I could, but no one had seen you since your neighbor stopped to talk to you this afternoon.''

"That was just before I got home. He was inside, waiting for me.''

"I figured. Anyway, we checked out Greenwillow and didn't find anything. The twins were okay, no one suspicious had been there, and we couldn't find your car.''

"My car.'' I would have to pick it up tomorrow. "It's parked off the road about half a mile from the hospital.''

"I know. One of the local cops spotted it while we were waiting. I didn't think Spanner would try to break in. I was expecting him to call and offer a trade, you for one of the twins. When he dragged you into the hospital, I started to see how he had managed it. Did he tell you much?''

"Only that Gerry Spanner was dead and buried and he had had a different identity for forty years.''

"It's probably true. I did a little digging today. He joined the army in the Korean War, which started a couple of months after the Talley murder. The records show that Private Gerry Spanner was killed in action. I started looking for survivors in his platoon to establish the facts and came up with a couple of likely KIAs, guys he could have changed identities with. Two of them were orphans.''

"You mean when someone else died, he switched dog tags and became someone else?''

"Either that or he killed someone, blew him up with a grenade so he couldn't be identified. Maybe Spanner even got himself lost for a while and then reported in as someone else to another unit where he wasn't known. There's always a lot of confusion after a major action.''

"What an awful life he must have lived,'' I said, "knowing every minute was a lie.''

"That was his choice. And he deserved a little agony. Look at what he did to a woman and her sons. He took away the most important person in their lives and then stole the next forty years from them.''

I nodded. I was beyond talking. It was closer to when I usually wake up than to when I usually go to sleep. Jack came up with me, kissed me, and went back downstairs. I had forgotten to ask if he was staying, forgotten to offer him a pillow. About all I could think of was closing my eyes.

29

I awoke about ten, smelling coffee. Jack was making breakfast when I got down.

"They gave me today off so we can clean up the mess up here. You'll have to make a statement to the local police today, and probably the county district attorney."

"Today I can do anything."

He bought some telephone cords, restoring my service. Then we went down to the police station and I told my story, which took a fairly long time. It seemed like there were a million questions. The story was, after all, forty years long. When we were finished, we had lunch.

"I also checked up on your favorite suspect, Patrick Talley," Jack said when we were waiting for our sandwiches.

I grinned at him. "What did you find?"

"Well, for openers, he was wanted by the FBI."

"Then he was involved in insurance fraud."

"They sure think so. But once he left for the Bahamas, that was the last they ever saw of him. And by the way, Mrs. Talley, if she's still alive, hasn't been back to the States in over fifteen years."

"Living the good life with her husband's ill-gotten gains."

"Looks that way."

I was still a little peeved that I had been wrong about Patrick. "It seemed so logical," I said. "No one had more to gain than he."

"Except Spanner. For Spanner, killing Mrs. Talley was a matter of life and death."

After lunch we drove over to Greenwillow.

Virginia must have seen us from her window, because she came out to the car. "I have some very bad news," she said.

I felt the cold chill. "What is it?"

"James has been hospitalized. They think it may be a heart attack."

I have a rather childish habit of pointing out facts to counter news of happenings I cannot deal with. "They slept through everything last night," I said, hoping she would tell me I was right and therefore what she had said could not possibly be true.

"The doctor thinks it may have been the effects of the poisoning, the anxiety of the last days. The truth is, men have heart attacks on golf courses and no one ever knows why."

"Is Robert with him?"

"They thought it would be better if he weren't."

"It isn't better." I got out of the car, feeling angry. "Doctors don't know everything. Where's Robert?"

She took us to the patio, and I introduced Jack along the way. Robert was sitting by himself with the old lost look on his face. "Come with me," I said, and he came along in his old docile manner.

We went to the cardiac unit, and I persuaded the nurse on duty to let Robert and me in. James was hooked up to half a dozen wires and tubes and seemed to be asleep. I held Robert's hand and we stood near the bed, not saying anything. About a minute passed. Then James's eyes opened and the twins looked at each other. Then there was a small smile.

I remembered what Dr. Courtland had said about Gerry Spanner's proposed experiments. He had wanted to see whether they functioned as savants when their backs were to each other, when they were certain distances away, when a wall was between them. I was convinced James had sensed his brother's presence in his sleep and opened his eyes to acknowledge it.

Robert sat on a chair and I walked away, leaving them together. The nurse, however, was insistent that Robert stay no longer then ten minutes. I tried to suggest having Robert sleep on a cot near his brother, but she wouldn't hear of it. I took Robert back to the waiting room where Jack was waiting, and we all walked back to Greenwillow.

One of my neighbors had stayed in the house to wait for the glazier, so when we got back, the window had been fixed. I walked into the dining room and saw my papers spread out. All that work, and now it was over.

"I feel at loose ends," I said.

"Looking for an excuse not to prepare for your poetry course?"

"No excuses." I started gathering my papers.

"Chris."

I turned from the table, and he put his arms around me.

"Think there'll be something there for us when we don't have the Talley murder to kick around?"

"I think so." It felt so good. "I know so."

"So do I."

That evening, alone and unafraid, I started through the poems. He was right about the old ones; they were all about love and death, but the best ones were love, and I felt a new appreciation of it. Lines that had once described something universal but not of my world now sang to me, all those blissful poets of four centuries ago, opening their hearts to their coy mistresses or coy loves:

> Clip me no more in those dear arms,
> Nor thy life's comfort call me,
> O these are but too powerful charms,
> And do but more enthral me!
> But see how patient I am grown
> In all this coil about thee:
> Come, nice thing, let my heart alone,
> I cannot live without thee!

Jack, my nice thing.

I fell asleep dreaming of the rapture of the contemporary American woman, myself.

30

The phone rang at seven-thirty Thursday morning.

"Chris, this is Virginia."

"Yes."

"I think you should come to Greenwillow."

"I'll be right there."

I chucked what was left of my breakfast and ran out to the car. A police car was parked in front of Greenwillow, and I ran to the door, feeling frightened.

Virginia was standing in the reception area, talking to two policemen. When she saw me, she left them.

"Come to my office," she said, leading the way.

We sat in chairs away from her desk.

"I got a call early this morning from the hospital," she began. "James died during the night."

"Oh no."

"Peacefully," she added, trying to smile. "I dressed and came here as quickly as I could. I knew Robert would have to be told, and I couldn't let anyone else do it." She paused and took a breath. "He died in his sleep."

"Robert?" I said. "Robert died?"

"Apparently so. We got the rescue squad here—they just left a little while ago—but he'd been dead for a couple of hours."

I closed my eyes, opened them, and shook my head rapidly, trying to clear it. Parts of a whole. When one died, the other could not survive alone. They had not been looking at each other or in the same room, and they had much more than a wall between them, but it had happened. They were gone.

"Have you called a priest?" I asked, my practical nature taking hold.

"Jonesy called the rectory of St. Mark's. He's on his way."

"I had hoped they would have many years in each other's company."

"They had a week. And you gave it to them. Someday you will think of that and it will be a comfort."

I was unable to answer. Brushing my tears away, I went upstairs to Robert's room to wait for the priest from St. Mark's.

I have had my share of delivering bad news. I have had to call parents of a student to say that their daughter was hurt in an automobile accident. I had to call a family to tell them that their beloved aunt, a nun at St. Stephen's, had passed away. Today I had another terrible call to make. I had to call Magda and tell her about her boys.

"This is Christine," I said when she answered.

"Christine." She sounded so happy to hear my voice. "And how are the two old gentlemen?"

Yes, I thought, how kind of her to see that they were boys no more. "I have some terrible news, Magda," I said, and then I told her.

The funeral was the next day at St. Mark's. Virginia and I agreed that it was best for the Greenwillow people to bury their dead quickly.

I sat between Gene and Magda, whom I had picked up in Queens. Gene held my hand through most of the mass, or maybe I held his. Maybe on this day I needed more comfort than my cousin did.

The mass in its constancy is a comfort in itself. Whenever I smell the incense I have a sense of the ages, of time, of continuance.

The Talley brothers could not have had a more devoted

group of worshipers at their funeral. My retarded cousin Gene and his friends seem to find it easier to love than to feel anything else—hate, dislike, even neutrality. Sitting in that pew, I could feel the love, and I knew that the twins must have felt it in the week they were at Greenwillow.

One week, after forty years.

31

On Saturday I drove to St. Stephen's. It was nearly two weeks since I had had my talk with Mother Joseph, and now I had to tell her both that she had been right and that the twins were gone. I had once entertained the idea of getting the three of them together, since Joseph was so largely responsible for the twins' reunion, but so soon it was too late.

I arrived at two, a quiet afternoon in summer. A novice walked across the grass near where I parked, her head down, her arms crossed, her hands tucked into her sleeves. Her life at St. Stephen's lay ahead of her. Today I knew that mine was behind me.

I went to the Mother House, saying hello to Grace, who was on bells. She called upstairs to tell Joseph I was coming.

The room looked exactly as it had at the time of my last visit. I was almost sure the same papers were atop the same piles on the long table. Joseph's office was like the constancy of the church. It irritates sometimes, but it can always be relied on.

She had coffee for us in one of those silvery pitchers that keep things warm, and she poured it into two rather lovely china cups. Then I told her the story.

I thought at times that I was dragging it out, prolonging it with too much detail, but each time I tried to rush through something, she slowed me down. I was in tears when I finished, and she came around the table and patted my back.

"Have you ever seen our view of the river?" she asked, her hand resting on my back.

"The legend of St. Stephen's?" I said, patting my eyes with a tissue. "Only in my dreams."

She opened the door to her closet and pushed back a raincoat and a couple of empty hangers. Then she said, "Follow me," and walked right into the closet.

It was fairly deep and lined with shelves behind the bar that held the hangers. On the shelves were paper, paper clips, ink, and other office supplies. At the rear of the closet was another door. Joseph pulled it open and passed through.

Following her, I came to a narrow set of stone stairs along the outside wall of the building. It was a long flight—her office had a very high ceiling, which I had taken to be directly underneath the roof—and at the top was a door. Joseph pushed it open and we entered a small room under the eaves with a floor of unfinished pine boards and walls of stone. Inset in the stone were two deep grooves that looked like gun emplacements in old forts.

I walked over to one and peered through it, and sure enough, there it was, the mighty Hudson in all its glory.

"Oh my God," I whispered, something I could not have said six months ago. "It's true then."

Joseph was smiling. "Great truths sometimes become great myths. Not many people have come up here. You're probably one of the few who wasn't a superior. But since you turned one myth into truth, I thought you deserved to see another."

"Thank you."

"Well deserved," Joseph said.

32

I moved into the master bedroom that night. With the mirror no longer an enemy, there seemed no reason anymore not to be more comfortable.

I spent Sunday with Jack, swimming at the private beach and cooking dinner together at the house. We acknowledged that we had great feelings for each other, but I told him it was too soon for me to make any kind of commitment to see him exclusively. I'm just too new at this, and I need to stretch my wings a little.

The mayor, of course, didn't even need my report since the whole thing was front-page news in the local papers. But he told me that an informal poll of the council indicated Greenwillow would be granted their variance. I expect them to move to Oakwood around the first of the year.

Gerry Spanner will probably live, but I expect he'll spend the rest of his life in prison. Although he will not be tried for the Talley murder, he will be tried for kidnapping—I was kidnapped—breaking and entering, carrying an unlicensed weapon, threatening police, and a hundred other things that all seem to go together. I will have to testify at the trial, which I don't look forward to, but it has to be done. I'm convinced he's responsible for the death of James, and therefore also of Robert. Incidentally, Jack's guess about Spanner's identity was right on the mark. The identification he was carrying was in the name of a man in his company in Korea. I expect the poor fellow's remains are buried in the Spanner family plot.

I spent a few days writing letters to people who deserved

to know what had happened—Dr. Sanderson; Arnold Gold, James's lawyer; the group home in Buffalo. The letter I got back from Arnold Gold was so thoughtful and considerate that I've decided to go into New York a couple of days a week and do some work for the causes he supports. It's the kind of thing I had in mind when I left St. Stephen's, and I think this is the place to start.

It turned out the twins did have a sizable inheritance, which was managed by some state appointee who didn't know an awful lot about the twins. Most of the money—aside from his annual fee—had been accumulating interest for all these years and had reached a staggering sum. Probably Greenwillow and the home in Buffalo will receive most of it. For Greenwillow that will certainly help the renovation of the house in Oakwood.

At the end of July I invited the whole block to an open house. As I was getting dressed, I opened the closet door and there was the yellow silk dress I'd been avoiding all summer. It was just perfect for the occasion. I didn't invite Jack, because he isn't exactly a member of the family yet. But all the neighbors came, including children, and we had a great time.

I made it an afternoon party so that the children would be able to come and also so that it would end early. By seven, the last of the guests had left. By nine I had cleaned up. By ten I was in bed.

I still get up at five o'clock in the morning.

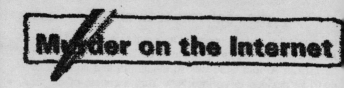